**GO AND
TELL MY CHILD
TO LET ME GO**

GO AND TELL MY CHILD TO LET ME GO

- Blondella James Brown -

ReadersMagnet, LLC

Go and Tell My Child to Let Me Go
Copyright © 2021 by Blondella James Brown. All rights reserved.

Published in the United States of America

ISBN Paperback: 978-1-956780-39-0
ISBN eBook: 978-1-956780-38-3

All rights reserved. No part of this publication may be reproduced, stored in a retrieval system or transmitted in any way by any means, electronic, mechanical, photocopy, recording or otherwise without the prior permission of the author except as provided by USA copyright law.

The opinions expressed by the author are not necessarily those of ReadersMagnet, LLC.

ReadersMagnet, LLC
10620 Treena Street, Suite 230 | San Diego, California, 92131 USA
1.619.354.2643 | www.readersmagnet.com

Book design copyright © 2021 by ReadersMagnet, LLC. All rights reserved.

Cover design by Ericka Obando
Interior design by Mary Mae Romero

Table of Contents

Introduction 1

1. Guilt and Shame 3
2. Forgiveness 6
3. Fear 15
4. Dealing with Worry 22
5. First Things First 25
6. Children and Family 36
7. Do's 40
8. Don'ts 42
9. Prison Ministry Guidelines 47
10. Sermon Excerpts: Divine Strategies for Survival 53
11. Good News for the Offender 63
12. Testimonies from Ex-Offenders Who Have Turned Their Lives Around . . . 68
13. Parent's Testimony 77
14. My Story 81
15. Confession of Faith 87
16. Conclusion 88

Bibliography 93
Glossary Of Terms 95

Dedication

To my loving husband, my sweet mother, prison ministry volunteers, chaplains, to all parents who have had a child or loved one incarcerated, and to all who have been incarcerated and searching for hope and restoration, never to walk this way again.

Acknowledgments

I am deeply indebted to a number of people in the preparation and completion of this book. They include the number of ex-offenders who shared their issues, problems, hang-ups, and blessings. I want to thank the parents and my personal friends of offenders who shared their experiences and emotions. Special thanks to Carol Hogan-Williams who encouraged me to tell my story. I thank Sadie Elloitt for allowing me to become a part of her volunteer prison ministry team. I also want to thank Dr. James Askew, who advised me on publication. I am grateful for the many authors who contributed valued information. Their books and publications are reflected in the bibliography.

Introduction

I am writing this book for several reasons. It is an expression of the many feelings and emotions that I experienced while on a journey in and out of prison (figuratively speaking) with my one and only incarcerated male child. I want to encourage parents to release their child from emotional attachments that can affect their health, finances, self-esteem, and relationship with God. I want them to trust God to relieve them of guilt and shame, fear, unforgiveness, and anything that holds them captive. I also want to encourage offenders and ex-offenders to understand how their incarceration has affected the lives of others while inspiring them to change by surrendering their lives totally to Jesus Christ. He is the only one who can break the cycle of bondage.

I want to address this book to every parent, grandparent, foster parent, or any person who has cared for a child and reared them in church, taken them to Sunday school on Sunday mornings, YPWW (Young People Willing Worker), Sunshine Band, Purity Classes, Christmas Programs, Easter Programs, AIM (Auxiliaries in Motion), Christian camps, or any church-related activities. This is also for every parent who has gone to football practice, basketball practice, soccer practice, band practice, track practice, including games, parent meetings, etc. I also want to include all the parents who have made financial, emotional, and spiritual sacrifices for the children.

Through the years, I have met many born-again believers, mostly women, who have sons, daughters, and other family members who are incarcerated or have been incarcerated. During the last Church of God in Christ Women's Conference that I attended, in May of 2011, one of the prayer warriors testified about her son who had been incarcerated. An altar call was made for all the women there who had incarcerated children. The altar was filled with women crying out to God in prayer and supplication for their children. These were women who knew the Lord, pastor's wives, missionaries, evangelists, Sunday school teachers, and women from every generation, from every walk of life, and from every social and economic status.

It was a very emotional experience. I could feel the pain, the hurt, the guilt, and the shame that these women were experiencing. I know firsthand what they were going through, because I've been there.

During the years that I have gone in and out of prisons and jails with my son, I've learned some valuable lessons along the way. I want to empower others and strengthen them through their experience, by inspiring parents and caregivers to seek forgiveness, be patient, and not accept guilt, shame, or fear. Turn your loved ones over to God. Have the faith, trust, belief, and confidence that God is in control. Stay prayerful and let God be God.

1

Guilt and Shame

The first time my son was incarcerated, I felt the worst guilt and shame that anyone could imagine. I felt that I'd failed as a parent and truly believed that I let God down by not training my child properly or helping him find the right path in life. He departed from my teachings, the Word of God, teachings from the Christian school, and all of the positive people around us who were so inspirational and encouraging in our lives. I was overwhelmed with guilt and shame. At that time, I felt God had made a terrible mistake in allowing me to become a parent. I loved my son dearly, but I had messed up as a mother.

In my mind, I tried to rationalize it away. I wanted it to be a dream that I would awake up from and put out of my memory, but it didn't happen. This was real and I had to deal with it. Only God got me through it.

I have since learned that guilt and shame are emotions that cause us to regress, hindering our spiritual growth. These emotions, along with fear, can lead to depression. It will leave us with a feeling of worthlessness. You may even question your ability as a parent.

Guilt and shame are two of Satan's most powerful weapons. He uses guilt and shame against us because they are effective in bringing us down, making us feel unclean, unworthy, and incompetent. This is an insult against our faith, trust, and confidence in God. We must remember that our Lord and Savior Jesus Christ died to free us from the bonds of sin, in addition to freeing us from the guilt and shame. Our spiritual victory depends upon us having a guilt-free conscience that flows from our trust in Jesus Christ. Paul encourages Timothy to maintain a pure conscience (I Timothy 3:9).

We may or may not have done anything wrong. If you make a mistake, own up to it and start to forgive yourself. When we own our mistakes, we can learn from them. Realize that we cannot undo what has already been done. Love yourself and move on.

Forgiving yourself makes it easier to forgive others. We must not allow our children or loved one's criminal behavior to hold us hostage. This is another trick of Satan.

As believers, we cannot allow ourselves to continue to think about how bad we must have been as parents. Satan loves to remind us of our past. When Satan tries to bring up our past, we can remind him that he has a past as well. He was an angel in heaven and was put out, so he wants to keep us out also. Stop thinking about what you could have, would have, or should have done differently. Our children and loved ones made bad choices that resulted in their prison incarceration. Paul tells us to forget those things in the past (Phil. 3:13).

As parents, as believers, and as human beings, yes, we will fail from time to time and make huge mistakes, because we have all sinned and fall short of the glory of God (Roman 3:23). However, we are not defeated by failure, and we will rise up and live on. Remember our relationship with Jesus does not give us immunity from trouble, failure, hurt, or pain. No matter what happens in our lives, God is still in control. We belong to God through faith in His Son Jesus Christ. We are to go through our battles in victory. Remember God did not promise us a life without problems, but He did promise to be with us through our problems. We are troubled on every side, yet not distressed; we are perplexed, but not in despair, persecuted, but not forsaken; cast down, but not destroyed. (2 Cor. 4:8-9).

How much more shall the blood of Christ, who through the eternal Spirit offered himself without spot to God, purge your conscience from dead works to serve the living God?

—Hebrews 9:14

Brethren, I count not myself to have apprehended: but this one thing I do, forgetting those things which are behind, and reaching forth unto those things which are before.

—Phil. 3:13

Forbearing one another, and forgiving one another, if any man has a quarrel against any: even as Christ forgave you, so also do ye.

—Col. 3:13

Come unto me, all ye that labor and are heavy laden, and I will give you rest.

Take my yoke upon you, and learn of me; for I am meek and lowly in heart: and ye shall find rest unto your souls. For my yoke is easy and my burden is light.

—Matt. 11:28-30

2

Forgiveness

In today's Christian circles, we hear a lot about forgiveness. All of us at some time in our lives have felt a need to be forgiven, or felt that we needed to forgive. Because we're humans, we struggle with anger, madness, frustrations, pain, disappointments, and hurts. We've also hurt others either knowingly or unknowingly. Nevertheless, the pain is there and it's real.

In our pain and suffering, we may find it hard to give and receive forgiveness. We've been hurt by that family member over and over again. You were once so close, but now just the mention of their name stirs up so much anger that it scares you, because you know that you are on the border of hate and contempt for that loved one. But since you are a Christian, born-again believer, saved from your sins, you just cannot stop loving that wayward son, daughter, father, mother, husband, wife, grandmother, grandfather, uncle, aunt, niece, nephew, or cousin, because after all, they are still family.

Being family makes it hurt the most. You gave them chance after chance. You took a chance with them when no one else would. You know that they were reared in the church and you know there is no excuse for their destructive behavior. You know deep down in your heart that you lived a godly life before them. You have cried and prayed, prayed and cried. You searched your soul for some sort of understanding, but there is none. After much soul searching, your heart tells you that you must forgive. You already know this, but the Holy Spirit confirms it.

You do not want to live your life without forgiveness in your heart. That is not an option for you, because you love Jesus. Unforgiveness can be like a cancer, and unless it is treated, it will eat at you until it has eaten you up. You've heard the expression, "He was eaten up with cancer, or the cancer took them out."

Unforgiveness is a spiritual cancer that is rooted in sin. It lingers in the heart and mind, and unless you root it out, it will take you out. Why serve God for years and years and then miss heaven because of unforgiveness?

In Luke 15:25-32, we have a parable within a parable. This is a classic story of a father forgiving a wayward son. The second parable is the story of a jealous, resentful, and angry brother who was upset that his father has forgiven his brother and welcomed him back home:

25 "Now the older brother was in the field. And as he came and drew near to the house, he heard music and dancing.

26 So he called one of the servants and asked what these things meant.

27 And he said to him, 'Your brother has come, and because he has received him safe and sound, your father has killed the fatted calf.'

28 "But he was angry and would not go in. Therefore his father came out and pleaded with him.

29 So he answered and said to his father, 'Lo, these many years I have been serving you; I never transgressed your commandment at any time, and yet you never gave me a young goat, that I might make merry with my friends.

30 But as soon as this son of yours came, who devoured your livelihood with harlots, you killed the fatted calf for him.'

31 "And he said to him, 'Son, you are always with me, and all that I have is yours.

32 It was right that we should make merry and be glad, for your brother was dead and is alive again, and was lost and is found.'"

The older son was apparently working and missed the initial reunion and did not know what was going on. He was on his post doing his job, taking care to be dutiful and responsible. When he returned to the house, he could smell the meat cooking and heard the music and laughter. He asked one of the servants what was going on.

When he heard what was going on, the drama began. He responded in anger, shouting and pouting. Then he refused to attend the celebration. He shouted, "It isn't fair, it isn't right. That boy should be run out of town, instead you are celebrating him. It's not fair!"

His father tried to reason with him, but to no avail. The older son tried to explain to his father how faithful, honest, trustworthy, committed, dedicated, and hardworking he had been all this time. He claimed to have done all of the right things, yet his father never once offered to give him a young goat (fatted calf) so that he might celebrate with his friends.

It was hard for the older brother to understand that being a parent means more than just treating each child equally, but it does mean that you treat each child fairly according to their individual needs. A parent's love is not based on a quota system, but on the individual child on a one-to-one basis. Maybe the older son understood that when he became a parent or maybe not.

The father finally reminded the son that everything he had already belonged to him. When we get to really know our heavenly Father, we will also realize that all that is His belongs to us. We have no reason or right to be resentful of whom God chooses to forgive or bless.

Remember that Jesus has a self-denying, deep, active, compassionate, merciful, and sacrificial love for the sinner. How deep is our love and how much are we willing to forgive?

I strongly believe that many Christians miss their blessing, their healing, real joy, and peace because of unforgiveness in their hearts.

"I forgive you" are some of the most powerful words in the English language. These words have literally changed lives. What impact did these words have on you when you realized that Jesus totally forgave your sins?

"I forgive you" is an expression of generosity toward the persons who have hurt us. It means that we release that loved one from the hurt and pain they have caused. We surrender our wounds to be healed and our hearts to be mended. Forgiveness is not for the one who has inflicted the pain, but it is for us. We need to forgive so that our heart can open again for God's love to flow freely through it.

My heart was broken to the point that I felt physical pain. It was a deep, piercing hurt. It felt like someone had thrust a knife into my heart and began to twist the knife as they plunged deeper and deeper. I knew that I needed to forgive—I mean really forgive from the bottom of my heart and not just through words from my mouth.

Unforgiveness left me angry, bitter, and hurt. My pride and self-esteem had been damaged. During this time, I continued to serve in the ministry while having to hide behind a mask and cover my pain with a smile. I had to pretend all was well with me, when deep down, it wasn't.

My biggest problem was I felt I didn't need to forgive because I didn't do anything wrong, after all, I wasn't the one who committed a crime and went to prison. My breakthrough came when I began to see forgiveness from a new set of eyes. I wanted my life to be better and not bitter. I made a life-changing decision to turn my hurt and pain over to God and allow time to heal. Today, I know I have totally forgiven and I am free from the hurt and pain through the grace of God.

One of my favorite stories of forgiveness is the Old Testament story of Joseph in Genesis 37-45. In the text, Joseph's older brothers were jealous of him. He was the son of Jacob who fathered him in his old age. It was obvious to his brothers that Joseph was very dear to their father. Joseph was treated special and given a coat of many colors.

One day in a jealous rage, his brothers put him in a pit, and then later, they took him out and sold him into slavery to a band of Ishmaelite travelers. Joseph ended up in Egypt. After a string of events, including a prediction of a seven-year famine, Joseph was elevated to oversee all of the pharaoh's affairs.

During this course of time, Joseph's brothers came before him, humbly begging and pleading to buy Egyptian grains so that their families would not starve. Joseph's brothers didn't recognize him, but he knew his brothers. Joseph not only offered them food, but he also offered them forgiveness. He held no anger, hatred, or resentment toward them. Joseph was able to forgive them and recognize the hand of God at work to save the Hebrew nation. Joseph was the second most powerful man in Egypt next to the pharaoh. He could have retaliated against the wickedness of his brothers' actions, but he waited upon God to work out His plans to restore His family. Joseph recognized the overriding power and providence of God at work in all the things that happened to him. He acknowledged that his brothers sinned, but he also saw God's bigger picture unfolding. It was not about Joseph, but it was about God's purpose and plan. Nothing can happen to a child of God that is contrary to His will. If Joseph missed that, then the story would have had a different ending.

Another one of my favorite Old Testament stories of forgiveness is the story of Job, who lost all of his children and livestock. He was stricken with sores from his head to his toes, and to add insult to injury, his wife suggested that he curse God and die. Then his friends came along and accused him of doing something against God, and that was why he was in that condition. In Genesis 42, Job repented and prayed for his friends. He forgave them. Then God restored Job's losses and gave him twice as much as he had before.

Sometimes, it may take years for us to understand the purpose and plan for our lives when bad things happen. Some things we will never understand in this life, but we can be assured of Romans 8:28. bold all things work together for the good to those who love God, to those who are the called according to His purpose. I emphasize the first four words because most people neglect to quote these words. These first four words are, in fact, the most important words of the scripture. **And we know that** are powerful words that should build our confidence in the God we serve. I stress these four words because it gives me added confidence and assurance that God is faithful. God will never fail. He knows all about me and whatever circumstances I am in. He has proven Himself to me over and over again. I know Him through experience, and whatever He brings into my life, He has complete control of it. All things, the good, the bad, and the ugly will work out for the child of God.

Another great story of forgiveness occurred in Acts 6 of the New Testament when Stephen, while being stone to death, asked God to forgive his murderers.

Stephen was set up by false witnesses and accused of blasphemy against Moses and God. After giving his accusers a history lesson, Stephen announced that they were stiff-necked and uncircumcised in heart and ears, resisting the Holy Ghost just as their fathers had done. They stoned Stephen as he called on God, saying, "Lord Jesus, receive my spirit." Then he knelt down and cried out with a loud voice, "Lord, do not charge them with this sin." And when he had said this, he fell asleep (Acts 7:59-60).

In the model prayer, Jesus admonished us to forgive our debts, as we forgive our debtors (Matthew 6:12; 14-15). "For if you forgive men their trespasses, your heavenly Father will also forgive you. But if you do not forgive men their trespasses, neither will your Father forgive your trespasses."

Jesus also teaches us that the spirit of forgiveness has no boundaries. In Matthew 18:21-35, He let Peter know that forgiving seven times may be a lot in his eyes, but in the eyes of God, seven is not enough. Jesus said, "up to seventy times seven." Four hundred and forty nine is not a magic forgiveness number. It simply means that forgiveness has no limits. If we are honest with ourselves and kept records of the number of times we needed to forgive, then it would probably reflect more than seventy times seven.

When we truly forgive, we don't even entertain thoughts of retaliation against our loved ones who angered and hurt us so deeply. Instead, we obey the words of Jesus in Matthew 5:44, But I say to you, love your enemies, bless those who curse you, do good to those who hate you, and pray for those who spitefully use and persecute you. We cannot hold grudges or anything against our loved ones or people in general. Jesus wants us to replace resentment, anger, disappointments, and disgust with love . . . for "love will cover a multitude of sins (I Peter 4:8)."

Jesus died to offer full forgiveness and pardon to everyone. At the cross, Jesus offered a priceless gift of forgiveness through His death, burial, and resurrection.

Jesus gave up His life in heaven to live among sin sick men in this world. Andre Crouch wrote a song that said, "He left his mighty home in glory to bring to us redemption story. I don't know why he sacrificed his life, but I'm so glad he did."

Jesus did amazing things here on earth, such as healing the sick, feeding the hungry, and casting out demons. He did nothing but good deeds, told the truth, and brought good news, yet he was falsely accused, lied about, beaten and scourged, crowned with thorns, made to carry His own cross half naked, mocked, taunted, and given wine mixed with gall to drink, all while Roman soldiers gambled for His robe.

Jesus did not deserve to die like this, because crucifixion was for criminals and Jesus was no criminal. In spite of all of His omnipotent power, he humbled Himself and became sin for the sinner. He knew that the world needed a Savior, for all have sinned and fall short of the glory of God (Romans 3:23).

His sacrificial death on the cross made it possible for us to be forgiven of our sins and our lives restored back into a right relationship with God the Father. Sin separated us from the Father. Jesus' atoning death forgave our sins and satisfied the payment for sin.

Because of our sins Jesus' death was necessary. Without the shedding of blood there is no remission (Hebrews 9:22).

God's love for us is so great that He sent His only begotten Son to die in our place. For God so loved the world that He gave His only begotten Son, that whosoever believes in Him should not perish but have everlasting life (John 3:16).

God loves us so much that when we have yielded to anger, bitterness, or grudges, He still forgave us. Remember, God wants us to lay those things aside and replace them with a heart of mercy and forgiveness. When we have experienced God's personal love, that's love.

When I was child, one of the things that helped me in life was my earlier teachings. My siblings and I were constantly reminded by my parents to treat other people the way that you would want to be treated. The way we treat others is the way God will treat us. We all want mercy and we have to offer it to others, especially our incarcerated children and loved ones.

We belong to Jesus. We were bought with a price. We must treat others right even when they mistreat us. Jesus taught us to forgive if we want to receive forgiveness.

Jesus wants us to forgive not just the bigger offenses, but the smaller ones as well. Jesus freely forgave us and He wants us to forgive freely. Remember what Jesus told Peter, "seventy times seven," and freely give what we have freely received.

Another example for us to follow is the parable in Matthew 18:23-25. A king wanted to settle his accounts owed him, and he showed mercy to a servant who owed him a large amount of money and wasn't able to repay him. The servant didn't have the money he owed so he pleaded with the king to be patient and have mercy on him. The king's heart was moved with compassion and he forgave the servant's debt. But the servant, on the other hand, also had someone who owed him a much smaller amount of money. Instead of the forgiven servant showing some mercy to his debtor, he forgot about the mercy that was shown to him.

When the king heard the news, he was angry. How many times have we gotten a case of amnesia? Like the king in the parable, God has written off the debts that we owe. Jesus, who owed no debts, paid the price for the debts that we owed and could not pay.

God expects us to show mercy to others. Even when we know they owe us so much, or when we find it impossible to forgive. We must ask God for the grace to help us forgive from the heart. We have to release that loved one from what they owe us and release them to God.

Sometimes, when we are hurt, we see through a different set of eyes. Our natural eyes are cloudy, and Satan will use this as a means of making us think that forgiveness is impossible or that our loved ones don't deserve to be forgiven. But this is not Jesus' way. Jesus was confronted by falsehoods, hatred, cruelty, abandonment, and opposition, yet he still chose to extend love, grace, mercy, and forgiveness.

Deep hurts, wounds, anger, frustration, and disappointments can spiritually, physically, and emotionally drain us. We must decide what position we want to take.

Forgiveness is not always easy, but without God's Holy Spirit, it is impossible. That's why we must pray and ask God to change our hearts. When we are sincere, God is faithful and will empower us to change and obey His commandment to love. He will enable us to forgive freely and unconditionally with mercy and compassion.

Therefore be merciful, just as your Father also is merciful. "Judge not, and you shall not be judged. Condemn not, and you shall not be condemned. Forgive, and you will be forgiven."
—Luke 6: 36-37

Thou hast forgiven the iniquity of thy people; thou hast covered all their sin. Selah.
—Psalm 85:2

As far as the east is from the west, so far hath he removed our transgressions from us.
—Psalm 103:12

If we confess our sins, He is faithful and just to forgive us our sins, and to cleanse us from all unrighteousness.
—1 John 1:9

Forbearing one another, and forgiving one another, if any man have a quarrel against any: even as Christ forgave you, so also do ye.

—Colossians 3:13

And when ye stand praying, forgive, if ye have ought against any: that your Father also which is in heaven may forgive you your trespasses.

—Mark 11:25

3

Fear

When we allow worry to set in, we open the door for other anxieties and we respond in fear. Fear is associated with sin. The first act of fear is recorded in Genesis 3:10, when Adam disobeyed God in the Garden of Eden. Fear was precipitated by sin. When God spoke, Adam responded, "I heard your voice in the garden and I was afraid . . ." God gave Adam the faith he needed to support his life. When Satan gained a stronghold on Adam, however, all of that faith was distorted. Satan still uses that distorted spiritual stronghold to cause fear, kill, steal, and destroy. The faith that Adam once processed in his heart was turned into fear. Adam knew that he was out of the will of God, so he hid himself.

Faith and fear work in opposition to each other, in that they produce opposite results. The law of reciprocals was at work here. God's Word is truth, and Satan's is a lie. Satan is the opposite of God, like good and evil, light and darkness, faith and doubt, saint and sinner, and belief or disbelief.

The Bible describes fear as a spirit. God has not given us the spirit of fear but of power, and of love, and a sound mind (2 Timothy 1:7).

When we are endowed by the Holy Spirit, we describe that as God's anointing. The anointing of God enables us to speak and act with boldness, power, authority, and confidence. The anointing of God causes Christians to do things that they would not do under natural power and strength. The anointing allows us to do supernatural spiritual things.

The spirit of fear does just the opposite. It brings about a negative and destructive effect. God's anointing will energize you, but fear will paralyze you. God's anointing will allow you to make sound decisions. Fear, on the hand, will confuse you and cause you to make poor judgments. The anointing of God will bring a blessing, but fear will bring a curse.

Fear is the opposite of faith. When our faith fails, fear sets in. An example of failed faith equating to fear occurred in the story of Jesus sleeping on a boat in the midst of a storm on the Sea of Galilee.

Matthew 8:23-27:

23 Now when He got into a boat, His disciples followed Him.

24 And suddenly a great tempest arose on the sea, so that the boat was covered with the waves. But He was asleep.

25 Then His disciples came to Him and awoke Him, saying, "Lord, save us! We are perishing!"

26 But He said to them. "Why are you fearful, O you of little faith?" Then He arose and rebuked the winds and the sea, and there was a great calm.

27 So the men marveled, saying, "Who can this be, that even the winds and sea obey Him?"

Why were the disciples so afraid? They were all in the same storm, but Jesus was able to rest while His disciples were terrified and fearful for their lives. The disciples were confronted with a different set of circumstances. The atmosphere of the storm, the strong winds, and the heavy rains caused fear for them. Their fear actually separated them from Jesus. Being in the storm caused the disciples to lose faith. Fear caused them to see death and not life.

They already knew what Jesus could do. They saw and experienced His various miracles over and over again. In the midst of the storm, however, fear caused them to see harm, danger, darkness, turmoil, discouragement, and failure. For a period, their fears blinded them from the delivering power of Jesus Christ. Fear became the opposite of faith.

Jesus let His disciples know that their fear attributed to their lack of faith, and their lack of faith was the source of their fears. Jesus demonstrated that faith and fear are interrelated. The Word of God produces faith. So then faith comes by hearing and hearing by the Word of God (Romans 10:17).

Satan uses the weapons of fear to disable believers. Fear has a negative effect on the believer as well as the unbeliever. It may manifest itself in several ways. Fear is one of the characteristics of the last days. "Men's hearts failing them from fear and the expectation of those things which are coming on the earth, for the powers of the heavens will be shaken (Luke 21:26)."

Fear factors are all around us. The world is encompassed by fear. We are afraid of nuclear wars, failing economy, slow economic growth, oil shortages, home foreclosures, repossessions, health care issues, cancers, air pollution, and contaminated waters, etc.

Overall, we are fearful of failure. We fear that we will not be successful by the world's standards. We fear rejection and that we will not be accepted by the world or those around us.

We must remember that all of our successes or failures are ultimately based on our relationship with Jesus Christ. He is the source of our strength. Even the fear of death should have no hold on the believer. "Death is swallowed up in victory (1 Cor. 15:54)."

The fear of isolation can make us feel lonely, forsaken, and forgotten by family, friends, and loved ones. We may sometimes feel lonely, but we are not alone.

The Word of God promises every believer, "I will never leave you, nor forsake you" (Hebrews 13:5).

Fear can become contagious by affecting the people around us. Satan uses fear to work through our senses. It manifests itself through our senses in the things we see, and the things we hear and touch.

We can depend on God to work through His Spirit by faith. Faith is the reverse of fear. It is the invisible. Now faith is the substance of things hoped for, the evidence of things not seen (Hebrews 11:1).

Fear can be caused by the very thing that we are familiar with. If we have experienced certain patterns of behavior, we may be inclined to anticipate a negative outcome. If we have experienced our loved ones as thieves, liars, deceivers, and questionable friends who are crafty, dishonest, unreliable, immature, and guilty of possible suspicious criminal activity, the thought of all those negative experiences can spark fear in us.

From my past experience, the results have not been favorable. Since we know firsthand what a loved one is capable of, it may initiate fear and anxiety. Sometimes, our fears may be justified, and sometimes, they have no merit at all.

Believers must be careful because fear can trick and deceive. Fear can have us imagining something that isn't real. Fear breeds the things we fear the most. It can become a self-fulfilling prophecy. If you fear death or dying by age thirty, for example, then you may be dead by that time.

While a loved one is incarcerated, we have complete control of our lives. Then the thought of them coming home will suddenly terrify us. It's a bittersweet feeling. You're glad they're getting out, but on the other hand, you're unsure of what to expect. Will you retain your power and control or will it be taken away?

When our loved ones are getting ready to be released, it can be a fearful and stressful time. Our fears may become exacerbated if we feel our loved ones may be out of touch with reality. Sometimes, they really are.

The fear of man will bring a snare into our life. It is a dangerous thing that can get us into some uncomfortable places. As believers, we must speak the Word to our fears. We must decide to walk in the power of God's love. When we walk in love, there is safety and protection.

Psalm 91:1-6:

1 He who dwells in the secret place of the Most High shall abide under the shadow of the almighty.

2 I will say of the Lord, "He is my refuge and my fortress; my God, in Him will I trust."

3 Surely He shall deliver you from the snare of the fowler.

4 He shall cover you with His feathers, and under His wings you shall take refuge; His truth shall be your shield and buckler.

5 You shall not be afraid of the terror by night, nor of the arrow that flies by day,

6 nor of the pestilence that walk in darkness, nor of the destruction that lays waste at noonday.

We can live and walk free from fear. When we have God on our side, fear will have no power or authority over us. The Lord is on my side; I will not fear: what man can do to me (Psalm 118:6)?

We must recognize that the source of our fear comes from Satan and it is not from God. For God has not given us the spirit of fear; but of power, and of love, and of a sound mind (2 Timothy 1:7).

Satan generates fear through various circumstances in our lives when we do not take authority over them by faith. When we listen to Satan and pay attention to his words, we leave ourselves exposed for fear to operate in our lives.

Fear will hold us hostage when we entertain Satan's words and not God's Words. Satan's words are destructive, and they're designed to take our focus off Jesus. We must continue to trust Jesus and His Word.

One night Jesus went walking on the water toward His disciples. First, Satan attacked them with a spirit of fear and they thought Jesus was a ghost. Jesus spoke the words, "Be of good cheer! It is I; do not be afraid." The moment the disciples heard the voice of Jesus, they were comforted and energized. Peter was so confident that he asked Jesus if he could come to Him on water. Jesus invited Peter to come. When Peter initially stepped out of the boat and had his focus on Jesus, he did just fine. But the moment Peter took his focus off Jesus and started to look at his surrounding circumstances, he became afraid and started to sink. He forgot for a brief moment to trust Jesus. Satan took advantage of that vulnerable moment and quickly fear set in (Matthew 14:22-31). Satan will seize every opportunity he can to challenge our faith.

The spirit of fear can take root in our lives and enslave us to fear. When the spirit of fear enslaves us, we are controlled by fear and not by faith. Just like a puppet on a string, fear can manipulate and dominate our lives. Not only will fear hold us in bondage, but anything that we allow to control us like alcohol, drugs, tobacco, sex, pornography, Internet, food, gambling, etc.

Your faith will free you from the bondage of fear. There is freedom in faith.

Satan knows that when he can activate fear in your life, that is a lack of faith. He wants to keep us bound so that we cannot effectively serve God or others. He disables us with the bondage of fear. It is out of order for a Christian believer to live in bondage. Fear is a sin and the Bible says, for whatsoever is not from faith is sin (Romans 14:23).

When we are born again of the Spirit, we become the children of God. The Apostle Paul said, For you did not receive the spirit of bondage again to fear, but you received the Spirit of adoption by whom we cry out, "Abba, Father" (Romans 8:15).

The Word of God assures us that believers should never fear. We can trust God and believe His Word. We can tell our fear that they will have no dominion in our lives because Jesus is with us to protect and help us. He said, "I will never leave you nor forsake you (Hebrews 13:5)."

God wants us to trust in Him. He will be there for us and He will help us. Put your trust in God and He will grant you the strength and courage to weather the storms in your life. Oh, taste and see that the Lord is good; blessed is the man who trust in Him! Oh, fear the Lord, you His saints! There is no want to those who fear Him (Psalm 34:8-9).

God invites us to trust Him because He desires to keep us safe and protected. God is faithful. Fear can have no dominion in our lives when we put our total trust in God. Whenever I am afraid, I will trust in you. In God (I will praise His Word), in God I have put my trust; I will not fear. What can flesh do to me?

Worry and fear are closely related. When we allow worry to set in, we open the door to invite other anxieties into our lives, and that is fear. Every sin has a doorway of entrance; we must keep the door closed. Fear opens the door for Satan to take up residence in our hearts. Then we respond in fear and not in faith. God wants us to trust in Him. He will be there to help us in the times of trouble.

We must be careful not to let Satan in. We cannot listen to his destructive words. No matter what we see, hear, or feel. Stand on the true, eternal, and unchanging Word of God.

Whenever I am afraid, I will trust in You. In God (I will praise His Word), in God I have put my trust; I will not fear. What can flesh do to me?

—Psalm 56:3-4

For God hath not given us the spirit of fear; but of power, and of love, and of a sound mind.

—2 Timothy 1:7

For ye have not received the spirit of bondage again fear; but ye have received the Spirit of adoption, whereby we cry "Abba, Father."

—Romans 8:15

There is no fear in love; but perfect love casts out fear, because fear involves torment. But he who fears has not been made perfect in love.

—I John 4:18

He shall cover you with His feathers, and under His wings you shall take refuge; His trust shall be your shield and buckler.

You shalt not be afraid for the terror by night, nor of the arrow that flies by day,

Nor of the pestilence that walks in darkness, nor of the destruction that lays waste at noonday.

A thousand shall fall at your side, and ten thousand at your right hand; but it shall not come near you.

—Psalm 91:4-7

Be not afraid of sudden fear, neither of the desolation of the wicked, when it cometh. For the Lord shall be thy confidence, and shall keep thy foot from being taken.

—Proverbs 3:25-26

In righteousness shalt thou be established: thou shalt be far from oppression; for thou shalt not fear: and from terror; for it shall not come near thee.

—Isaiah 54:14

In God have I put my trust; I will not be afraid what man can do unto me.

—Psalm 56:11

Be of good courage, and He shall strengthen your heart, all you that hope in the Lord.

—Psalm 31:24

So we may boldly say: The Lord is my helper; I will not fear. What can man do to me?

—Hebrews 13:6

4

Dealing with Worry

Every person who has had someone close to them incarcerated probably had some concerns about that person. Some concerns are natural; however, when our concerns become excessive, that is worry in disguise. Cain asked the question, "Am I my brother's keeper (Gen. 4:9)?"

Any Christian with the heart of God should have some concerns for their brother, sister, son, daughter, grandchild, niece, or nephew. When that concern becomes worry, it blinds us to the realities of God's care for us.

I grew up in a very nurturing home where my mother was always caring for someone. She cared for my father, sisters, brother, grandmother, great-aunt, and neighbors. God has made women caregivers by nature. That innate nature follows the incarcerated. Often we don't realize the concern that we have for that person remains with us even though that person is out of our sight, but not out of our hearts.

While our loved ones are incarcerated, worry can affect us in several ways. Worry can affect the quantity and quality of our lives. It can wear us out and wear us down. Worry can affect our physical and emotional health. It can diminish our immune system, which can inhibit us from fighting off colds, flu, fevers, allergies, or pneumonia. According to Dr. Charles Mayo, co-founder of the Mayo Clinic, worry affects the circulatory system, the heart, glands, and the nervous system.

Worry can affect our spiritual health because it keeps us from hearing God's voice. Jesus warns, and the cares of this world, and the deceitfulness of riches, and the lusts of other things entering in, choke the word, and it becomes unfruitful (Mark 4:19).

Worry will steal our joy in the Lord. The joy of the Lord is our strength. Worrying will take the joy out of our hearts. Our hearts and minds become focused on the person and not on the presence of God. This can cause destructive anxiety and undue stress on our lives. It affects our relationship with God and other people in our lives as well.

The story of the two sisters Mary and Martha clearly illustrates how worrying can affect the people around us. When Jesus and His disciples stopped by their house to eat, Martha scrambled around the house cleaning and getting things ready for the meal. But her sister, Mary, sat quietly and still at the feet of Jesus listening to His teachings. Martha was so bothered and frustrated at Mary that she began to complain to Jesus. "Lord, don't You care that my sister has left me to serve alone? Tell her to help me."

It was clear to Jesus that Martha was irritated at her sister's lack of interest in domestic chores. His response probably surprised her when he said, "Martha, Martha, you are worried and troubled by many things. But one thing is needed, and Mary has chosen that good part, which will not be taken away from her (Luke 10:40-42)." In other words, Martha was majoring on the minor, and minoring on the major: Martha was focusing on things that were unimportant and insignificant, while Mary was focusing on the most important thing, which is sitting at the feet of Jesus, hearing His words.

It is important that we not let worrying take us away from the presence of God. Worrying is an indication that we no longer believe in or trust Him. This is a negative position to be in.

We must remember that God is our God. We have a personal relationship with Him and we can put our total trust in Him.

When worry comes in, the most important thing we can do when worry tries to attack us is to develop a heart of thanksgiving. When we have a thankful spirit, the peace of God will fill our lives. The peace of God will allow us to take the focus off our problems and situations and give ourselves completely to the very presence of God. The spirit of thanksgiving says that we can totally and completely trust God to work things out for our good. When we listen to God, He promises to give us peace. He will give us inner peace that comes from our trust in Him.

I will hear what God the Lord will speak, for he will speak peace to His people and to His saints; but let them not turn back folly.

—Psalms 85:8

And let the peace of God rule in your hearts, to which also you were called in one body; and be thankful.

—Colossians 3:15

Thou will keep him in perfect peace, whose mind is stayed on you, because he trusts in you. Trust in the Lord forever.

—Isaiah 26:3

Trust in the Lord with all your heart, and lean not to your own understanding; in all your ways acknowledge him, and He shall direct your paths.

—Proverbs 3:5-6

Trust in the Lord, and do good; dwell in the land, and feed on His faithfulness. Delight yourself also in the Lord, and he shall give you the desires of your heart.

Commit your way to the Lord, trust also in Him, and he shall bring it to pass.

—Psalms 37:3-5

Remember that God is in control, no matter what Satan tries to do to us. He controls the good, the bad, and the ugly. And we know that all things work together for good to those who love God, to those who are the called according to His purpose (Romans 8:28).

Let us align our hearts with the promises of God by being thankful for His presence in our lives. Thank God for His Son Jesus who promises to give us perfect rest from worrying and complete peace.

Come to Me, all you who labor and are heavy laden, and I will give you rest.

Take my yoke upon you and learn from Me, for I am gentle and lowly in heart, and you will find rest for your souls. For My yoke is easy and My burden is light.

—Matthew 11:28-30

5

First Things First

I am very grieved by the fact that the recidivism rate is so high in our state's prison system. There are far too many people returning. For some it seems like a revolving door. They have come in and out and out and in. Before the computer can process their numbers out of the system, they are right back in the system again. They stay put like window dressing.

This reminds me of how the children of Israel wandered around in the wilderness for forty long years, when in fact it was only an eleven-day journey into the promised land. Right before Israel's possession of the promised land, Moses warned that they were at the mountain long enough. In other words, the children of Israel wandered around long enough and it was time for her to become a settled nation (Deuteronomy 1:1-8). God had already prepared the promised land for Israel. Like He did for Israel, God has already prepared for us everything we need to be successful by faith through the shed blood of Jesus Christ.

When a person repeatedly goes back to prison, they are labeled as institutionalized. This simply means that the person becomes so comfortable in the prison system that they will actually sabotage their freedom. Some may act out before their release and get in trouble. Then when they are released, they may do something crazy like committing another crime and doing the same old things that got them there in the first place, which results in a trip back to prison. This is a sick behavior, but it is real.

Some are looking for answers in all the wrong places. There is only one true and real answer. You will never have to use your lifeline for the right answer. The real answer is Jesus. He is the question and the right answers.

This reminds me of going to the doctor sick and the doctor does not know what's wrong with you. He performs a series of test to rule out what is not wrong with you. My brothers and sisters you have tried a series of things to make you feel better, yet you can find no lasting comfort, no relief, no peace, no joy, no satisfaction, and no lasting happiness in any of it. You have tried legal or illegal drugs, like acid, PCP, LSD, heroin, ecstasy, oxycontin, marijuana, crack, or cocaine, alcohol, fast cars, fast women, gambling, shacking, un-shacking, marrying, and remarrying. You name it; you have tried it and then some. You have done it all and still none of it worked for you.

You think if you have enough money and that's all that you need. The truth is that you can have money and still feel broken down. Money is not the answer to your problem. Money can buy you a state-of-the-art hospital room in a state-of-the-art hospital, but it cannot buy your health. Money can buy you a lot of love and happiness, but it cannot buy inner peace. Only Jesus can give you a peace that surpasses all understanding. He'll give you lasting real peace even without a dime in your pocket.

You have resisted a relationship with Jesus long enough now. You have tried to find yourself in other religions, but you still felt empty and disconnected. My brothers and sisters, it is time for you to make a decision to follow Jesus today. Decide today to accept Jesus Christ as your Lord and Savior. I know that you have said to yourself that you've got time. But the bottom line is that time is no longer on your side. We actually have less time today than we had yesterday. Jesus is on His way back and the countdown is getting lower every day.

Become a follower of Jesus today and you will not regret your decision. First, realize that God loves you so much that He sent His only begotten Son to redeem us from our sins and offer us eternal life in heaven (John 3:16). God intended for believers to have eternal life. Eternal life means a life spent forever in heaven with Jesus and the Father when we die. Heaven is only available to those who have accepted Jesus into their lives as Lord and Savior.

Contrary to belief, you will not automatically enter into heaven when you die. Mama, granny, auntie, and even the preacher might try to put you there, but it will not happen. Heaven is a holy place reserved for holy people. Only those who have accepted Jesus and live a life of obedience to Him will enter into heaven.

The reason we need Jesus in our lives is because of sin. Sin first entered into our lives in the Garden of Eden when Adam disobeyed God. Sin entered in and separated us from God. All mankind was born in sin and fall short of the glory of God (Romans 3:23).

When we sin, we are disobedient to God and commit wrongful acts. There is a consequence for sin or any wrong act such as breaking the law. The Bible teaches that the wages of sin is death, but the gift of God is eternal life through Christ Jesus our Lord (Romans 6:23). Our sins separated us from God and if we die in our sins, we will be separated from God forever in a place called hell. Hell is a real place prepared for Satan and his angels. It enlarges itself daily, so do not become a part of that reconstruction plan.

God required that a blood sacrifice be made for sin. In the Old Testament, the priest offered the blood of animals as a sin offering. In the New Testament, God sent Jesus as a pure, clean, holy, and sinless sacrifice for the sins of mankind. Jesus was the only one qualified for the job. He was the perfect sinless sacrifice. God wrapped Himself up in sinful like flesh and entered into the womb of a virgin named Mary.

Jesus came into this world not to condemn the world but that the world through Him might be saved (John 3:17). We cannot save ourselves by living a good life. For by grace you have been saved through faith and that not of yourselves; it is the gift of God, not of works, lest anyone should boost (Ephesians 2:8-9).

None of us are perfect or good enough. We cannot go to heaven by joining a church or getting baptized. None of our human efforts can connect us back to God. They all come short.

There is only one way to God the Father in heaven and that way is through His Son Jesus Christ. Jesus is the only one who can save us from our sins and restore us back to God. Jesus said, "I am the way, the truth, and the life. No one comes to the Father except through Me (John 14:6)." The only way we can get into the family of God is by way of Jesus. There is no other way.

God has proven His love for us by sending Jesus to die for us, even while we were still living in sin. The Bible says, But God demonstrated His own love toward us, in that while we were still sinners, Christ died for us (Romans 5:8). When Jesus died on the cross and rose from the grave, He paid the penalty for our sins, so that we can have life. Jesus has already paid the price. It is up to you to accept what He has done.

STEPS TO SALVATION

In order to come to Jesus, you must first begin to trust Him by faith as your Lord and Savior. In order to trust in Christ, you must believe that He is the Son of God who died to forgive us of our sins. Now you are ready to invite Him into your heart: Behold, I stand at the door and knock. If man hear my voice, and open the door, I will come in to him, and will sup with him, and he with me (Revelation 3:20).

When we receive Jesus, we become children of God and He becomes our Heavenly Father. The Bible says, But as many as received Him, to them gave power to become the sons of God, even to them that believe on His name (John 1:12).

Accepting Jesus is the most important decision of your life. Take this decision very seriously. If you are willing to accept Jesus Christ into your life today as your Lord and Savior, please pray this prayer:

Dear Lord, I know that I am a sinner, and that I have sinned against you. Please forgive me of my sins and cleanse me from all unrighteousness. I believe that Jesus Christ is your Son and died on the cross for me. Come into my heart and from this day forward, help me to live for You, serve You, and obey You. Amen.

1. Admit that you are a sinner.

For all have sinned and come short of the glory of God (Romans 3:23). Confess that you are a sinner and ask God to forgive you of your sins. When we ask God's forgiveness, it means that we are willing to quit and discontinue our sinful ways with God's help. If we confess our sins, He is faithful to forgive us our sins, and to cleanse us from all unrighteousness (1John 1:9). Once we confess, God does not hold our sins against us. Satan may try to bring them up or accuse you of being unworthy of forgiveness. But remember, the Bible says that our sins will be cast into the depths of the sea (Micah 7:19).

2. Confess your sins and repent.

Confession is followed by repentance. Repentance means to turn or to change from your sinful ways. Sin and unrighteousness separated us from God, and now confession and repentance will turn us toward God. Confession and repentance work together. Repent of your sins and trust Jesus as your Savior. Repent means to be godly sorry for your sins and turn to God for forgiveness. You are now ready to turn from your old ways of living, and turn to God's way of living. Repent therefore and be converted so that your sins may be blotted out . . . (Acts 3:19). When we accept Jesus into our lives, we also accept a new way of living. When God cleanses us, He gives us a new nature. Our desires will be to please God and not ourselves. Therefore, if any man be in Christ, he is a new creature: old things are passed away; behold all things are become new (2 Corinthians 5:17).

There was an old song that said, "I went to the church one night and my heart wasn't right, but something got a hold of me. I looked at my hands and they looked new. I looked at my feet and they did, too, and ever since that wonderful day, my soul's been satisfied."

Conversion should change you. Your hands and feet will not literally change, but your heart will. Hands that used to cheat, steal, rob, fight, abuse your spouse, roll marijuana joints, and shoot dice don't do these things anymore. Those same hands are now lifted up in worship and praise. Feet that used to go in and out of the hotel, motel, or Holiday Inn with someone else's wife or husband, now stay home with your own family. Lips that used to bad mouth the preacher are now his armor bearer or head deacon. Instead of talking about what the preachers are doing with the money, you are now a tithe payer and cheerful giver. Instead of making excuses about going to church, you now take action and bring your family to church. Instead of throwing the Bibles that the prisoner volunteers brought into the trash, you are now a prisoner ministry volunteer. You know that Jesus made the difference in your life and you can gladly share your story with others who are incarcerated. You can witness to the changing power of the Gospel of Jesus Christ, because you have been there, and you have done what they have done and then some. Your life is a witness and you are happier than ever knowing that you are walking and talking with Jesus.

3. Make a decision today to commit to serve God with your whole heart.

Now that you have decided to accept Jesus Christ into your life as your Lord and Savior, you are saved. You may not look different, but you should feel different. Satan will come to try to convince you that nothing has happened, that you are the same, and that nothing has changed. But do not accept his lies. Remember he is the father of lies. He may try to tell you that your crimes were too many or too horrendous, and that you will never be forgiven. Do not accept this because they are all lies. The Bible declares as far as the east is from the west, so far has He removed our transgressions from us (Psalms 103:12). Jesus forgives us and does not hold our sins against us.

Do not doubt Jesus' finish work on the cross, just accept it by faith, humbly submit yourselves to Him, and allow Him to work in your life. Now that you belong to Him, let Him have complete control of your life.

You have served Satan long enough and all he ever wanted to do is kill, steal, and destroy you, but Jesus came that you may have an abundant life. Jesus said, The thief cometh not, but for to steal, and to kill, and to destroy: I am come that they might have life, and that they might have it more abundantly (John 10:10).

You will strive to live a Spirit-filled life each day with God's help. Remember you are not your own now, you belong to Jesus. Forasmuch as ye know that ye were not redeemed with corruptible things as silver and gold . . . But with the precious blood of Christ . . . (1 Peter 1:18-19).

You will **need** to become actively involved in a Bible-believing church. Your local church is important. It is beneficial for you to be in the company of other believers. There is strength in numbers, and they will be there to encourage you until you are able to stand on your own. The early church recognized the value of worshipping and fellowshipping together. It gave them strength and courage. There are many strong prison fellowship groups within the system. I have met many humble, honest, faithful, dedicated, committed, Spirit-filled, active, prayerful Christians behind bars. I have also met some missionaries, deacons, anointed musicians, and card-carrying ordained preachers who are incarcerated. They are on fire for Jesus and are not ashamed of the Gospel. Let us remember that we are all sinners, just saved by His precious grace. But we are all as an unclean thing, and all our righteousness are as fifty rags (Isaiah 64:6) . . . And let us consider one another in order to stir up love and good work, not forsaking the assembling of ourselves together, as is the manner of some, but exhorting one another, and so much the more as you see the day approaching (Hebrews 10:24-25).

When you find a church, meet with the pastor, and just be honest and up front with him. Let him know that you have just been released from prison and that you are a born-again Christian now and that you need their help in getting back into society and serving God. A good place to start is mama's or grandmother's church. They have relationships there, and some of the members may still remember you. This is just one option. The main thing is to find a Bible-believing, Bible-teaching church as soon as possible. The first thing you should do first is visit your parole officer, and then find a church. There may be men in the church who can also assist you with job leads.

Finding a church is also very important because of police checking up on you, or "police heat." There is little or no "police heat" within the church. The church also provides a type of insulation for you. You are now very vulnerable in your neighborhood. If there is a crime committed, you will probably automatically become a suspect. The police already know that you are out on the streets. If you are in the church, you are less likely to become a suspect. On the other hand, if you frequent the drug houses or clubs, the "police heat" will be there also.

If a crime does take place, you can honestly testify that you were in the service or Bible study during that time. It is a comfort knowing that you were not involved this time. Your church family will verify that you were there worshipping. Be careful where you go and how you manage your whereabouts. You already know which areas are high risk and which areas are not, and church is one that would be considered a low risk area.

4. Study your Bible and pray every day.

Remember, you are no longer in a controlled environment, and the challenges and temptations will be there to greet you. This is why prayer and studying the Word are so important. Serving God means believing what He says. The Word of God is truth. In order to know God, understand Him, and believe in His promises, you will need to regularly study His inspired Word. There are hundreds of Bibles in the chaplain's office just waiting for your I-60 to request one. An I-60 is a form the inmates can use to make a request from the chaplain of anything of a spiritual nature. For example, an offender may use an I-60 to request a Bible or inspirational materials or rosary, change denominations, become a part of a Bible study group, join the choir, speak with the chaplain, or phone call home. Believe me, every chaplain would be delighted to issue a Bible to every offender upon their request.

Paul encouraged Timothy to study to show thyself approved unto God, a workman that need not to be ashamed, rightly dividing the word of truth (2 Timothy 2:15).

When you read the Bible, ask God to reveal to you an understanding of His most Holy Word. All scripture is given by inspiration of God and is profitable for doctrine, reproof, correction, and instruction in righteousness, that the man of God may be perfect, thoroughly furnished unto all good works (2 Timothy 3:16-17).

The Word will strengthen you and empower you to resist temptations. Satan works full time, part time, and overtime. He will come after you because you no longer belong to him, but you belong to God. Therefore, submit to God. Resist the devil and he will flee from you (James 4:7). The only way to successfully resist the devil is with the Word of God.

The Word of God is just one of the most important tools that you will need to live the life of a committed believer. The Gospel of John is a good place to start. If you do not understand everything at first, just be patient. Pray for an understanding and revelation of the Word.

The Word of God tells us who God is, what He is like, and how to please Him. The Bible is our owner's manual of life. If you purchase a new phone, car, appliance, or home electronics, you will receive an owner's manual with that new item. It tells you how to use that item to get the most satisfaction and results. This is one of the ways that the Word of God works in our lives. If we follow it, the Word of God will enrich our life forever, while preparing us to live eternally.

In addition to studying the Word of God, you will need a consistent prayer life. Prayer is a way of communicating with God, and God communicating with you. It is a way of experiencing the power and presence of God.

Begin by acknowledging and reverencing God. It does not matter how long your prayers are as long as you pray from the heart in sincerity and humility.

Another important component of our salvation is praising God. One of the reasons that King David found favor with God was the fact that David was a person who loved to praise Him. He loved to praise God and give honor to Him. Praise allowed David to become a man after God's own heart. God wants us to praise Him. He is worthy of our praises.

Praise benefits the believer emotionally, psychologically, and spiritually. Praise helps us to be overcomers. It helps us to move into the act of worship. It connects our spirit man with God's Spirit. Praise helps us prepare our hearts for the Word.

We must get into the habit of praising. It unites the body of Christ in ushering in the Spirit of God to do His miracles and wonders. Our praises can create the right atmosphere for the Holy Spirit to move in. This also creates an atmosphere for God to answer our prayers.

It can help us to enter into the presence of the Lord and help others to enter into the presence of God. Praise prepares our heart to move into worship. The process of worship is designed to carry our praise and worship into heaven. It prepares the minds of the congregation to be ready to experience the move to God.

Praise prepares us to hear and recognize the voice of God. Personal prayer, praise, and worship create an atmosphere for us to learn the voice of God. Knowing the voice of God is an important step for the believer.

Believers are in a constant battle of spiritual warfare. Praise prepares us to fight in spiritual warfare. It can be a spiritual weapon that helps us with spiritual deliverance, drive out demons, and close the passageway for demonic activities. It is designed to be a spiritual offensive and defensive weapon.

Praise and worship will cause us to move into intercession for ourselves, ministries, cities, communities, and the world. Develop the attitude of praise and worship as part of your daily walk with God. It will strengthen you and it will make such a difference in your spiritual walk.

If it is possible, you may request to be baptized. Some chapels have baptismal pools and some may not. It will depend on where you are. I can recall once when our team was ministering at the women's unit in Gatesville, Texas, we actually used a horse's water trough. It served the purpose. I recall another incident when we were baptizing the women and the water was ice cold. We were concerned that the women might get the flu or pneumonia because the water was so cold. We started to pray and God miraculously warmed the water. It was amazing.

Note that baptism is not a prerequisite to salvation; however, in the Bible, Jesus commanded His disciples to be baptized. "Go therefore and make disciples of all nations, baptizing them in the name of the Father, and of the Son, and of the Holy Spirit. Teaching them to observe all things that I have commanded you; and lo, I am with you always, even to the end of the age (Matthew 28:19-20)." Jesus was baptized by John the Baptist, and His Father in heaven declared that He was well pleased.

When the Church started, new converts who became Christians were baptized shortly after their conversion (Acts 2:41). Remember baptism does not save you, because you can go down a dry devil and come up a wet one. Baptism is merely a public expression of your inward conversion.

Finding a job is also a priority and it may be a difficult task, but you can do it. Your parole officer may have some good job leads. Don't be afraid to ask people on different jobs in different places if they are doing any hiring. Word of mouth is an excellent job resource. You may be rejected, and it will not feel good, so don't take it personally. Rejection has happened to all of us at some time or another. Jesus was despised and rejected, a man of sorrow who was acquainted with grief (Isaiah 53:3).

Carefully manage your free time. This initially, will be a challenge for you. As I have mentioned earlier, you will no longer be in a controlled environment where prison guards are there to tell you what, how, and when to do something. With God, you can make it.

Stay away from the people and places that may jeopardize your freedom. Your homies may want to take you drinking, drugging, and clubbing. Let them know that you no longer engaged in that kind of lifestyle anymore. At first, they may not believe you or will even try to test you. They will only remember you from the last time they saw you in their world. Now you have a new way of thinking and doing.

Invite your homies to come and go to church with you. Let them see and experience you worshiping and praising God. Prayerfully ask God to show you how to witness to them. Each person will be different. Witness to what you know and have experienced. Remember, they are watching your new lifestyle. Always let them see Jesus in you, no matter what.

Before I accepted Jesus into my heart, I was an addicted marijuana smoker. All the people I knew were marijuana smokers. If you didn't smoke, then we didn't have anything in common. I smoked whenever I could and as much as I could. When I got saved, Jesus took the taste away instantly. I told my friends that I didn't smoke weed any more. I didn't have to worry about leaving them, because they left me. Then Jesus sent some saved friends into my life who were real friends that didn't smoke or drink, who helped encourage me in the Word of God and holy living.

You will not miss them or even realize that they are gone. Even though you have a different lifestyle now, you must continue to show them love. Don't be condemning or downgrade them. Don't forget that you were once where they are. God showed you grace and mercy. God said, I have loved thee with an everlasting love: therefore with loving kindness have I drawn thee (Jeremiah 31:3).

When you do see your homies, don't start talking about the things that you used to do and the places you used to visit. Remember, Satan loves to glorify sin! He will make sin look and feel so good. He will get you out on a limb and be the first to cut the limb off. Don't go there with them, because you will open up a door that you may not be able to close. When your homies want to revisit your criminal past, prayerfully ask God to give you the wisdom to redirect the conversation toward the saving grace of Jesus.

Remember to make a list of rules and understand that they must be followed when you come home. Do not talk about old people, places, or things. Talk only about positive things, like getting back in school, getting a job, making things right with your family and loved ones, or doing some volunteer work until you get a permanent job. If you don't have access to a computer, go to the public library or community centers in your neighborhood. Make sure that you follow up on your probation or parole as needed.

6

Children and Family

There are many things that need to be done, but you can only do one thing at a time. Do not try to move too fast. I know that some things may feel like they are urgent, but trust me they are not. You cannot reverse time so don't try. You cannot change your past, but you do have control over your future by the choices you make.

While you are incarcerated, stay involved with your children. It will be a challenge, but it can be done. It can be very difficult to remain a part of their lives. You might get a visit with your children or you might not. When you do get a visit, cherish those precious moments. You may or may not get to talk to them on the phone. If you don't get to visit or talk to them, it is still possible to maintain a positive relationship with them while giving them fatherly or motherly support.

Angel Tree, a program of Prison Fellowship, offers some helpful advice. They suggest that you become an expert on your child's stages of growth. Find out what they are learning, what subjects they are studying in school, and what activities they are involved in after school. Find out their grades, conduct, and compliment them on their achievements.

Take note of their likes and dislikes. Learn all that you can about their favorite subjects and discuss those with them. Look for free materials that can be sent to them.

Always remember to respect your child's father or mother (not your baby's mama or baby's daddy). Maintain a good relationship with them even if you are not together. Be respectful. The way a father treats his child's mother will teach them volumes about love and respect. If you are married to your child's mother or father, show the utmost love and respect. Fathers, love your wife as Christ loves the church, mothers love your husband. Your male children will learn firsthand how to treat women and females in their lives. Your daughters will also learn what is expected of a male.

Continue to maintain your relationship with Christ. You will need Him to get through this. You cannot make it without Him. Stay active in Prison Fellowship. Take advantage of the inspirational and teaching materials available through the chaplain's office. Take this time to get rooted and grounded in the Word of God.

Take care of your health; eat healthy and stay away from junk foods and starchy foods. If you are diabetic, eat right and take your meds. If you have high blood pressure, stay away from salt and greasy foods. Don't abuse your body. Remember, you need to be around for your children and family.

Drop the hard-core façade. Don't be afraid to share your emotions with your children. It takes nothing away from who you are.

Let your children know over and over again that you love them and have great expectations of them. If they mess up, try to show some compassion. Pray and ask God to give you the wisdom to have the right things to say. Cover them with prayer daily.

Be open and honest with them. Admit that you've messed up, made a terrible mistake, and ask for their forgiveness. They need to understand what forgiveness is all about. It facilitates healing and restoration for both of you. Use language that is age appropriate and don't talk over their heads.

If your unit offers a parenting class, sign up for them. Learn all that you can about being a parent, especially an absent one. The more you learn about parenting, the better you will become. We are not born good parents, but we can learn.

As an absent parent, you can still inspire within your child a desire for success. According to The Parent Institute, a child's desire for success is what motivates them to become self-disciplined and take responsibility for their own learning and behavior. When a child has a desire to succeed, they will become involved in activities that interest them. They will also have less discipline problems at home and at school. The drive for success must come from within. Remember that every child is different and unique in their own way. They are all wonderfully made.

Whenever possible, through their visits or by way of letters, take every opportunity to build their self-esteem. Always let them know that you love them, because knowing this is very important to their self-esteem. Let them know that they can do anything that they make up their minds to do. Encourage them to memorize I can do all things through Christ that strengthens me (Phil. 4:13). Encourage them to read and even study the Bible. The more they read, the more they learn.

Warn them about peer pressure and children who may think that being a brainiac is not cool. Let them know that there are more smart kids out there and they are not alone so keep on working hard. Also let them know that having good behavior in school and at home is the most important thing that they can do for you. If they are doing well in school, getting good grades, and staying active in extracurricular activities, that will make the time away from them much easier for you.

When they visit or write you, pay attention to what they are saying by being a good listener. When they are talking, you may just nod to let them know that you are listening. Many times, they will not need you to solve a problem, but just listen. Let their visits be quality time, and don't worry about the quantity of time.

Take advantage of the Angel Tree program. The Angel Tree is a win-win for inmates and participating donors. The program was started by an ex-offender named Mary Kay. Mary was a safecracker, bank robber, and one of America's Most Wanted. When convicted, she was initially given a one hundred and eighty-year sentence of which, by the grace of God, she only served six years. During her time of incarceration, Mary noticed that during Christmastime, the inmates were only able to give their children little toiletry items such as toothpaste, soap, or lotion. Some of the items were not even wrapped in Christmas paper, but the children were so happy and eager to get something from mama. The gift was not that important, but it was the thought behind the gift. It was just important and meaningful to them that they got something from the one they loved.

When she was released, Mary organized a group of volunteers and that first year collected over five hundred toys for children whose parents were incarcerated. The toys were given to the children on behalf of their incarcerated parent.

That following year, Angel Tree spread to twelve states. This is a perfect opportunity for churches to get involved in missions, evangelism, and church growth. The churches get an opportunity to interact with children and families. The congregational volunteers are doing something tangible in the community, and God is glorified. This is also a church possibility for the offender when they are released. Thank God for Angel Tree and its volunteers.

7

Do's

1. Do visit your loved ones.

If it is at all possible, do try to visit your loved ones. Nothing will lift an incarcerated person like a visit from family, friends, or loved ones.

There are some things you will need to remember when making a visit. Always remember to bring valid photo identification. You will also need lots of coins. You will not be able to give the inmates money; however, you will need the coins for the vending machines. Most of the inmate's visits are a maximum of two hours. You should also call ahead to make sure that you are on the visitor's list.

Do not try to pass contraband (anything the inmates are not allowed to have) to the inmates. It is not worth you losing your visiting privileges or worse, being arrested. Contraband may or may not be illegal for a free world to possess, but it is against prison regulations. Contraband includes, but is not limited to cell phones, chargers, money, drugs, alcohol, weapons, etc.

Remember, if you are going to travel a distance to visit, you may want to call ahead to check to see if the unit is on lockdown. Lockdown occurs when a major violation has been uncovered. Most of the time, only a few inmates are found in violation, but the whole prison will still be punished. When this happens, no one can move, except for a few inmates like the ones who have kitchen duty. Even the volunteer prison ministries are cancelled for a period of time.

Lockdown can be a difficult time for the inmates. First of all, many feel that it's unfair because they have not done anything wrong. They miss the visits that they were really looking forward to. They get no commissaries, no TV, and no recreational activities, etc. Every meal consists of a Johnnie (a cold sandwich) and no one is pleased.

I once took a trip to visit my son that was many hours away, and when we arrived at the prison gate, the guards turned us around and we were told the unit was on lockdown.

When the unit is on lockdown, it does not matter if you have traveled from as far away as the moon, you will not get in.

Lockdowns may occur if there is a riot, suspicion of weapons, potential escape, gang-related violence, drugs, phones, chargers, contraband, and so on.

This is disappointing and frustrating, since you have spent money for gas, sometimes money for a hotel or motel room, including your sacrifice of time, energy, and commitment. Remember to turn it into praise because it still could have been a lot worse.

I remember the very first time I went to visit my son, he was not on lockdown, but he was in some small Texas town that I had never heard of. It took several hours to get there. When I saw my son for the first time in those prison clothes, I just broke down and cried like a baby. I guess I had been holding it in, and the sight of him just opened up the flood gates. That was the hardest thing for me to see. He and I had been together for a long time. It was just the two of us. I realized then that my son was no longer my son, but he belonged to the state of Texas. A feeling of grief came upon me, and I felt that he was gone as if he passed away. I was weak and felt as though I would pass out. It's still painful to think about it even now.

When you visit, do remember to wear the appropriate clothes. Try to wear dark clothes, because the inmates all wear white, and you do not want to be mistaken for one of them. Do not wear clothes that are too revealing because you may be refused a visit. Be prepared for a full-body search. Leave your cell phone in your vehicle.

8

Don'ts

1. Don't give up on your child.

It may be difficult to trust them, understand them, or even believe what they have to say. You will probably wonder what is wrong with them. You may ask yourself on more than one occasion, "What did do I do wrong?" You may wonder, "Why is this happening to me?" You may more than likely try to remind God how much you love Him or how hard you have worked to help build the church, led others to Him, or worked on kingdom building. You will reflect on how you brought your child or loved ones up in the church to love God and the need to accept His Son Jesus as their Lord and Savior.

I made financial sacrifices to send my son to Christian schools. I worked at one of the schools as well. There were times when I would work three jobs to support us. I was a single parent at the time, and I got no support from his father. I did what I could for him to grow up in a Christian environment.

Satan will use people around us, even our own family members, to try to persuade us to give up on our loved ones. You may hear statements such as, "He's never going to change, or I told you he was no good, or he will always be up to no good." This is when we should respond to those statements with increased faith and prayer.

When our adversaries are being negative and cruel, ask them if they are praying or invite them to join you in intercessor prayer. They will start praying or they will keep quiet. Parents please remember to keep your child on the prayer list. Never, never, stop praying and believing God.

God is still in control and we can trust and believe in Him. His words will never, never, ever go void, but will accomplish what they are designed to do (Isaiah 55:11). We don't know how God is going to do it, but keep believing He will do it in His own time. Just keep believing God will do it and will be glorified in it. God is worthy of our trust.

He will create a way to come through, because He is the ruler of this universe, a big and sovereign God.

2. Don't abandon your church responsibilities or Christian duties.

Your child or loved one may have gone astray, but we must continue to remain faithful. One of my mother's sisters was a holiness pastor. She lived in the home with my grandmother who was the church mother. It was a very religious home. My grandmother would pray every day at noon. They were in the church every time the doors opened. Her son also went to prison. My aunt was so hurt and devastated that she contemplated resigning her position as pastor. She felt that she was such a failure and a disappointment to God. This is a trick of Satan to try to make parents feel like failures. Don't allow yourself to accept those feelings. When you know beyond a shadow of a doubt that you have done the best that you knew to do, then you have nothing to be ashamed of.

When my son was first imprisoned, I was weighted down with guilt and shame. I was convinced that I was a failure and unfit parent. I was depressed, and I could not figure out what I had done wrong. During that time, I was working as a chaplain intern at M. D. Anderson Cancer Hospital in Houston. I was helping others get through their pain and I needed help getting through my own pain. God brought me through, and He will bring you through.

Our children and loved ones are not the first who were brought up in the church and Christian environment to have gone astray or left the faith for the world. In the Old Testament, I Samuel 2:12-17; 22-25; 3:11-14, Eli, the priest had two sons who were brought up in the temple to serve God and they went astray. When the people brought a sacrifice offering, it was the custom of the priest's servant to only get certain portions of the offerings. The rest was to be removed and offered up to God. Eli's sons were taking what they wanted first and giving God the leftovers. The sons even had women in the temple for sexual pleasure.

Eli was fully aware of their ungodly behaviors. He was a godly man, but he made the mistake of not honoring God by allowing his sons to be corrupt in the temple. God allowed Eli's sons to be punished because Eli honored his sons more than God.

Parents, we cannot put our children or loved ones before God. He must be first in all of our lives. Nor can we allow them to do ungodly things and ignore it. No one should knowingly be allowed to get away with ungodliness in God's house. We cannot control our children's behaviors, but we must take a stand when it pertains to God, His people, or His house.

3. Don't put up a bond to bail your child or loved ones out of jail.

When a person is arrested, he or she may have an opportunity to pay a bail and leave jail until their trial date. The amount of bail will of course depend upon the nature of the crime. If the crime is too horrendous, no bail will be set. This is to ensure the courts that the accused will be there to appear during trial. When the courts issue a bail and the accused bail out, they are in essence, agreeing to appear in court at a future date and time. The amount of the bail is more than likely more than the accused can pay by themselves. This is when you will need the service of a bail bond company. The accused is charged 10 percent of their actual bail. The bail bond agency will put up the rest of the bail.

The 10 percent bail bond fees are usually non-refundable to the person who put up the bail. Most bail bond agencies will require the 10 percent plus collateral depending on the amount of the bail and the nature of the crime. The collateral is refundable back to the person who put up the bail.

Depending on the amount of the bail, sometimes collateral has to be put up. For example, if the bail is $5,000.00, the 10 percent ($500.00) is paid up front in cash. The remaining $4,500.00 needs to be given to the bail bond agency as collateral. This process guarantees the agency their money. Collateral may also be required if the accused is a repeat offender, flight risk, or may not show up for court.

Collateral may be in the form of credit cards, vehicle titles, personal assets, and mortgage or property deeds. The collateral works in favor of the agency to ensure that they recover the money they put up in court to secure the accused's release.

Once the accused persons make all of their court appearances, the court will refund the original bail back to the bail bond agency. Actually, this is how the bail bond agencies make their profit. This is known as a surety bond used to guarantee the entire bail amount if the accused maintains the terms of their release.

The advantage of bail bond is that the accused can go home if they make bail. They can continue to work on their jobs and provide for their families and it frees up overcrowded jails.

Your child may cry, plead, and beg you to get them out of jail. I really do not advise it. Because if you put up the 10 percent (you will not get it back) and collateral and they go to court as scheduled, more than likely, they will be found guilty and have to do the time.

I do realize that we do love our children with all of our hearts, but if we are not careful and fail to use wisdom, they will try to talk us into putting up our homes as collateral for them. My son tried it. This is a very bad idea, because if that loved one fails to appear for trial or sentencing, or jumps bail, you will forfeit your collateral, which may mean losing your valuables, property, or homes. Remember that God has not blessed us with homes, property, or valuables to be used by sinful activities. Love them but remain sensible.

4. Don't put yourself in a financial bind.

Do not put yourself in a financial hardship or feel guilty about not sending your loved ones money. Sometimes, when I worked in the office as a volunteer chaplain, I would monitor the inmate phone calls. I was appalled at how some of the inmates talk to their elderly parents. First, they request a phone call on the pretense that they have not heard from the parent and they pretend to be so worried and concerned about them. All they really want to do is beg for money and pretend they are hard up. Most of these elderly parents are on a fixed income; some have injuries and are not able to travel. It takes a very selfish person who tries to drain an elderly parent. Inmates get free room and board, blankets, linen, shoes, socks, haircuts, and hygiene items. All of them probably want to wear free expensive clothes and designer accessories to match, but that's not going to happen. Trust me, they make it without them. I know that my son liked to play basketball, and occasionally he would ask for some extra money to buy a pair of tennis shoes. I didn't have a problem with that. I would generally send him around $20.00 per month, which is about $5.00 a week and sometimes less. I wanted to make sure that he had enough money for stamps and envelopes. I wanted to hear from him and I didn't want any excuse for not writing. Parents, you don't have to send your child or loved one a lot of money. Remember, prison is punishment. The state is already taking care of them. Some of them will have a room full of snacks. You don't have to spoil them while they are in prison. You should not have to take care of an adult.

9

Prison Ministry Guidelines

1. Be yourself.

Don't put on a façade. They will recognize it in a minute. Many of these offenders have been conning most their lives, so they know a fake when they see one. Going behind bars for the first time can be intimidating. Hearing the resonating sound of iron doors closing behind you can really get your attention.

2. Be an understanding friend and good listener.

It is possible that you may become a volunteer mentor to an inmate. Don't share your personal business with them, but be there for them.

3. Be honest and sincere.

We don't know all of the answers so we must be honest and sincere. If you don't know something, or don't have an answer, just admit it, or you can tell them that you can try to find an answer if it is not against prison policy.

4. Be consistent and dependable.

Be punctual and arrive at the time you are scheduled. If you have committed yourself, follow through with it. If you can't make your commitment, be sure and let the chaplain know so that the inmates will not be expecting you, and that the chaplain can make other arrangements.

5. Be willing to learn.

Become familiar with the prison ministry guidelines in your state. Learn about the various state bills and legislations that may affect a person while they are in prison or out. Each state's laws will vary.

6. Be prepared for reality.

Have a plan and stick to it. You may arrive on time and not be allowed to minister. You may be stopped in the middle of the service for an inmate count, or an inmate may be called out in the middle of a service. Things happen, be prepared, but also be flexible.

7. Always be respectful of and work with the facility chaplain and the correctional facility administration and staff.

The guards can become your best friends. They can assure that the inmates will be ready for service on time and that the worship centers are set up. They make sure the services are announced, and if you have a good relationship, they will work with you and assist you in any way possible or may even allow you extra time for ministry.

8. Dress appropriately.

Dress appropriately for ministry. Don't wear anything too revealing, tight, flashy, or churchy. Be careful not to wear perfumes or fragrances that are too seductive.

9. Know and follow the rules of the institution.

Always know and follow the rules of the various institutions. Each facility may be different. If you visit more than one facility, some basic rules are the same, but each facility may operate autonomously. What you are allowed to do on one unit may not be allowed on another.

10. When in doubt, ask.

If you are not sure about something, don't make assumptions, just ask.

11. Develop the trust and confidence of the staff and administration as well as the inmates.

You will need them to be on your side and their support is invaluable.

12. Honor your commitment.

Do what you say that you will do. Remember the warden, chaplain, guards, and inmates are all depending on you.

13. Respect confidentiality.

Do not share inmate's information.

14. Be there at your appointed time.

If the guards announce that it is time to leave, then leave. Whatever you are doing or in the middle of, then stop, unless you are given special permission to continue. I realize that you are ministering; however, we are on the state's time, under their rules and regulations, and on their property, on their units.

15. Be cautious.

Do not allow an inmate to try to persuade you to do something that you're not supposed to do. Sometimes, they will try you. Many of them are professional cons and master manipulators. They know how to give you a believable story.

16. Make sure that you have permission to distribute Bibles or other Christian materials before you do so.

Anything that you bring into the prisons or jails to distribute must be approved first. I realize that you would love to bring in literature and Bibles to inspire the inmate; however, we must still follow rules.

17. Encourage the inmates to study the Bible and enroll in correspondence courses.

There are lots of free Bible study courses available.

18. Always invite the inmates to pray with you.

If you are praying in a group, be observant, because when your eyes are closed, some may be trying to touch or pass things around.

19. Talk to the inmates about general topics as well.

Find out what the inmates are interested in and discuss it with them, especially if you are mentoring.

20. Don't get caught up in an ego trip.

Don't try to debate or argue with them. Just redirect the conversation.

21. Do not make promises that you cannot or will not keep.

Assure them that you will do what you can. Do not offer false hope.

22. Don't run errands for inmates or act as go between.

Don't send money or anything else to inmates.

23. Don't bring anything in or out from an inmate without checking with the prison authorities first.

Some things are very harmless to us, but may be considered contraband for the inmates. For example, chewing gum may be used by inmate to jam locks.

24. Don't ask about an inmate's crime.

The inmate's crime should be of no interest to us, because we have all sinned and fall short of the glory of God. They got caught and we didn't. We have not arrived yet, because all of our righteousness is nothing more than a filthy rag.

25. Don't get involved in the inmates' legal problems.

We are not in prison ministry to address legal issues. There are channels for that. Our main focus is the proclamation of the good news of the Gospel Jesus Christ.

26. Don't give out your personal address or phone number.

Use the church address or post office box.

Be watchful of notes passing, inappropriate touching, or other suspicious activity. Remember that all of the inmates present may not be there to worship. The reality is that some inmates will come to the service just to get out of their cells. Some come thinking that they may get an early parole, or that it will look good for them when they go before the parole board.

Remember that if you have not been able to reach your child or loved ones, someone else may be able to. You may also be able to reach someone else's child or loved one. When your child gets saved, only God will get the glory. One waters, one plants, but God gives the increase.

Some of these prison ministry guidelines were adopted from S.K.I.P. (Saints Kids in Prison). The Saints Kids in Prison Ministry was founded in September 1999, by Carole

Hogan-Williams, for the sole purpose of getting the Gospel of our Lord and Savior Jesus Christ into the prisons of America, which houses our sons and daughters.

The SKIP Ministry is a ministry designed and developed by COGIC (Church of God in Christ) members for COGIC members that will address the many spiritual and rehabilitation needs of our incarcerated children. However, the SKIP Ministry Program can be adopted by any denomination to meet the needs of any children who are incarcerated or have been incarcerated.

The SKIP Ministry Program offers
Life Skills Training
Substance Abuse-12 Step Recovery Classes
Faith-based Marital Classes
Faith-based Parenting Classes
Anger Management Classes
SKIP Prison Prevention Programs
Spiritual Awareness Training
Understanding the Bible Classes
The Battlefield of the Mind Classes
Experiencing God Classes
Inspirational Book Club Discussion Groups
Job Readiness and Vocational Training
Resume Preparation and Interviewing Skills
Basic Reading Skills
Construction Vocational Training
Automotive Vocational Training
Computer Vocational Training
Correspondence Services
Aftercare Programs

These are just some of the many programs available through the SKIP Ministry Project. According to SKIP, prisons across this country are filled with our children primarily because of crimes related to drugs and alcohol abuse. What happened to our children may be due to a combination of factors such as neglect, single-parent homes, poverty, poor family environments, lack of education or job training, or even a church that failed them.

The nature and climate of racism also plays a major factor in the incarceration rate. According to the Statistics on Prison Population Rates, the racial make-up of prison inmates in the United States is highly disproportionate with Black males in America. Although Blacks comprise 12 percent of the US population, they represent over 40 percent of the inmate population. One out of every one hundred African American males is in jail, which is five times more than white Americans. The rate of incarceration is steadily on the increase. More than one in three Black males without a high school diploma is incarcerated.

Once our children leave the prison system, we must be prepared to care for them as they reenter society. The greatest destructive force against our children is their unconverted hearts and minds. Without the transforming power of the Holy Spirit, our children are lost in their sins, without hope and a true knowledge of the living Savior. They must be born again.

With God's help, we can help our children. Somewhere along the way, we have let them down, but we cannot just forget them or turn them over to the prison system. The burden to reclaim our children should not be on the parents alone. The twenty-first century church must help carry this burden as well. We are our brother's keepers. Programs such as SKIP Prison Ministry, various reentry programs, and other nonprofit Prison Fellowship organizations play a vital role in the rehabilitation of ex-prisoners.

10

Sermon Excerpts: Divine Strategies for Survival

Jeremiah 29:11-13

For I know the thoughts that I think toward you, saith the Lord, thoughts of peace, and not of evil, to give you an expected end.

Then shall ye call upon me, and ye shall go and pray unto me, and I will

Hearken unto you.

And ye shall seek me, and find me, when ye shall search for me with all your heart.

Traditionally, during the first of the year, we all make resolutions. We make New Year's resolutions in order to add improvements to our lives. New Year's resolutions are statements we make to resolve to do something better this New Year than we did last year.

New Year's resolutions are a good thing, but most of the time, we seldom keep them, or we may keep them for a week or two if that long. Some of the most common resolutions: I'm going to lose weight, stop smoking, stop drinking, or stop procrastinating. We can go on and on.

I have learned down through the years that in order for me to keep my resolutions, I need a plan. I need a strategy, I need goals, and I need a purpose. I want to encourage you to get a plan and develop some strategies for achieving your goals or your resolutions.

God has a plan. He has a plan for your life and for my life. Our text today was written by the prophet Jeremiah, who was one of the major prophets. He prophesied to the people of Israel that God was going to punish them because of their rebellion, unfaithfulness, and disobedience toward Him. The people did not like Jeremiah's message; they even called him a traitor. They mocked and taunted him because they did not want to receive what God was saying to them through his servant. Jeremiah cried all the time because the people were so insensitive to the God of their fathers. He was nicknamed the "weeping prophet."

Jeremiah was so discouraged that he told God that he was not going to speak His name again. After a while, the more Jeremiah tried to keep quiet, he just couldn't help himself. He said that the Word of God was just like fire shut up in his bones. When you know that God is good, you've just got to tell it. Jeremiah couldn't stop calling on the name of God because God had a plan for his life and a purpose for his life. The Mississippi Mass Choir sings a song that said, "I just can't stop praising His name, Jesus." God told Jeremiah that He already knew him before He formed him in the womb. God said that He sanctified him and ordained him even before the foundation of the world.

How many of you know that God has a plan for your lives as well. He has a divine strategy for our lives. God said that before Columbus sailed the ocean blue, before African slaves came to America, before Blue Bell ice cream, I knew you, and I have a plan for your lives.

Just as God has a plan for your life, Satan also has a plan for your life. His plan didn't just start when you were born. It started in the Garden of Eden when Satan beguiled Adam and Eve, by tricking and deceiving them into disobeying God. That one act of disobedience polluted and contaminated the entire human race. For all have sinned and come short of the glory of God (Romans 3:23). Satan walks around like a roaring lion seeking whom he may devour (1 Peter 5:8). He is a thief who wants to steal, kill, and destroy you, but Jesus said that He has come that we may have life and have it more abundantly (John 10:10).

God has a plan for man's survival here on earth. In order for you to be successful in the New Year, you will need a survival plan or survival strategies:

1. Accept Jesus into your life as your Lord and Savior.

Psalm 116:12-13, says, What shall I render unto the Lord, for all His benefits toward me? I will take up the cup of salvation, and call upon the name of the Lord.

2. Put God first in your life.

Seek ye first the kingdom of God and His righteousness and all these things will be added unto you (Matt. 6:33). Make Him number one. Love the Lord with all your heart and your soul. Get connected to God through His Son Jesus.

4. Ask God for direction for your life.

Trust in the Lord with all your heart, and lean not to your own understanding; in all your ways acknowledge Him, and He will direct your path. Learn how to trust in God (Proverbs 3:5-6). Learn how to depend on Him. Learn how to put your faith and confidence in Him.

5. Learn how to forgive.

We want God to forgive us and we need to learn how to forgive others. Forgive those who have wronged you. And forgive those whom you have wronged. God has forgiven our sins and carried them to the cross. He has taken our sins away and will not hold them against us, because He has thrown them in the sea of forgetfulness to remember them no more.

6. Repent.

Get godly sorrow down in your heart and turn from your sinful ways. Repentance is important because you are going to turn from your wicked ways to godly ways. Repentance will bring about a spiritual transformation in your life. Repentance will make a difference in you. When your heart is changed, God can change your mind. He can change your old way of thinking. Start thinking godly thoughts, righteous thoughts, holy thoughts, pure and clean thoughts. Let this mind be in you that is also in Christ Jesus. Take on the mind of Christ. Become Christ centered and not self-centered, because self-centeredness will get us in trouble. Don't go back to the same places or things you left. If you haven't smoked in years, don't start when you go home. Your body is the temple of God. Keep your temple clean.

7. Stay prayerful.

The Bible tells us to pray without ceasing (1 Thes. 5:17). Don't stop praying. Keep on praying and praying. Prayer is one of the most powerful weapons you have. Use it. We should consider it an honor and privilege to be able to go to God in prayer.

8. Don't go to God whining, begging, or complaining.

But go to God in the spirit of praise and thanksgiving. Learn how to praise and worship God. Be a thankful and grateful person. Be thankful in everything. Thank Him for your good, your bad, and your ugly. Remember, God didn't just arrest you, He rescued you, and saved many of your lives. Now He has given you another chance for salvation and eternal life.

8. Develop a daily appetite for the Word of God.

Study His word, mediate on it, live by it, and hide it in your heart so that you will not sin against God (Psalms 119:11). God's Word will keep you, protect you, and give you deliverance, love, peace, joy, and happiness. His Word will make a difference in your life and empower you to live victoriously in the coming New Year and years to come.

9. Become a person of action.

Don't procrastinate. You can have the things that God has for you. If you want to change, you must become a person of action. We can have the things that God has for us, but we must become people of action. We have a responsibility to do something. Faith without works is dead (James 2:26). Write your goals down, put them in writing. Look at them every day. This is your plan of action, this is your strategy. Write the vision and make it plain (Hab. 2:2). Without a vision, the people perish. Trust God. Don't let Satan steal your dreams. He is a dream stealer and a dream killer.

10. Don't be a quitter.

Jesus was not a quitter. Tell your neighbor, "I will not quit. I will not give up." And if you make a mistake, don't be afraid to start over. If you get rejected, don't take it personally. Jesus was rejected and despised of men. He will never leave you nor forsake you.

In closing, I want to remind you that just as Satan has a plan for your life, God has an even greater plan for your life. His plan or strategy is for you to live and not die. His plan is for you to have eternal life.

In the fullness of time, God sent His only Son Jesus. He searched the heavens and the earth. He looked at His servant, Abraham, a man of great faith. But when He looked at Abraham's résumé, he was a liar. Abraham would not do.

He looked at Moses, who led the children of Israel out of Egypt, but Moses was a murderer. He looked at David, a man after God's own heart. But David had too much blood on his hands. He was adulterer and a murderer. He looked at Paul, who wrote almost half of the books of the New Testament, but Paul persecuted the saints and he was an accessory to the murder of Stephen. He looked at Peter, but Peter was a hothead and carried a switchblade. God found no one worthy to take away the sins of man. But Jesus stepped up and said, "Father I'll go." Jesus is the Father's divine strategy for redeeming mankind.

In His divine strategies, He investigated our circumstances. He realized our guilt, weighed our burdens, witnessed our weaknesses, observed our hopelessness, saw our helplessness, and completed the plan of Salvation. Jesus comprehended our sorrows, inventoried our mistakes, surveyed our valleys, measured our mountains, calculated our losses, counted our failures, visualized our destiny, and moved with compassion toward us.

Andre Crouch said, "He left his mighty home in glory to bring to us redemption story. I don't know why he did, but I'm so glad He did." His divine strategy was to provide a solution to our sin problems and make everlasting life available to those who put their trust in Him. He came with a plan to give us a future and a hope.

Sermon excerpt: "You have been at this mountain long enough."
Deuteronomy 1:1-8

How many of you gentlemen here today think that you are in need of a change in your life in some way or another. Every hand in here should go up. If you want to change, change must begin in your mind. You must first change the way you think and then you will change your attitude.

Most of us want a change, but few of us are willing to do what it takes to change. We say that we want to change with our mouths, but we don't follow through with our actions. Proverbs 23:7 says, For as man, thinks in his heart so is he. When you think about things in your mind then that is what you will pursue. For example, prison ministry is always on my mind. Whenever I prepare a sermon, my thoughts are always on how I can shape the message for the prison ministry.

God already has a wonderful and prosperous plan for our lives. He desires that you prosper and be in health even as your soul prospers (3 John 2). God already provided everything that we need to be successful. The good life that God prepared for us has already been provided for us through the shed blood of Jesus Christ.

Turn in your Bibles with me to Deuteronomy 1:1-8, and the word of the Lord reads These are the words that Moses spoke to all Israel on this side of the Jordan in the wilderness, in the plain opposite Suph, between Paran, Tophel, Laban, Hazeroth, and Dizahab. It is eleven days' journey from Horeb by way of Mount Seir to Kadesh Barnea.

Now it came to pass in the fortieth year, in the eleven month, on the first day of the month, that Moses spoke to the children of Israel according to all that the Lord had given him as commandments to them, after he had killed Sihon king of the Amorites, who dwelt in Heshbon, and Og, king of Bashan, who dwelt at Ashtaroth in Edrei.

On this side of the Jordan in the land of Moab, Moses began to explain this law, saying, The Lord our God spoke to us in Horeb, saying: 'You have dwelt long enough at this mountain. Turn and take your journey, and go to the mountains of the Amorites, to all the neighboring places in the plain, in the mountains and in the lowland, in the South and on the seacoast, to the land of the Canaanites and to Lebanon, as far as the great river, the Euphrates. See, I have set the land before you; go in and possess the land which the Lord swore to your fathers, to Abraham, Isaac, and Jacob, to give to them and their descendants after them.'

My subject for today's text is, "You Have Been at This Mountain Long Enough." In our text today God was trying to prepare Israel for His gift of the promise land. The children of Israel had finally come to the end of their forty-year wandering period. God delivered them from out of 400 years of Egyptian bondage. God made the initial promise to their forefather Abraham that He was going to free the Israelites from their bondage. They cried out for a deliverer and God sent Moses.

Many of you have cried out for a deliverer. God sent the chaplain, Joy and Peace Ministry, volunteer chaplains, and numerous other ministries, but just like Israel, you are still wandering.

Israel wandered around for forty years and eleven months, almost forty-one years. The amazing thing about this experience was that it was just an eleven-day journey, just an eleven-day trip.

Some of you started out on a short stay, but it extended into years and years because of your behavior. Israel extended her trip because of her behavior. This is not new.

Here Moses was telling the Israelites that it was now time for a wandering people to become a settled nation and enter into an entirely different lifestyle. He began to mention some of the things that God had done for them, but he could not mention it all and neither can we. God has done so much for us we just cannot tell it all.

In verse 6, Moses reminded the children of Israel that they dwelt long enough on this mountain. In other words, Moses said to Israel that she had been in the same place long enough now, and it was time to move. It was time to make a change in their way of living.

Some of you have wandered in and out of this system and not moved into the promised land that God has for you. You have wandered in and out of Texas Department of Criminal Justice (TDCJ) long enough now. You have been from one end of Texas to another.

Brothers, it time for you to get yourselves together. When we look around at the level of violence today, and all the things that are happening in the world both nationally and locally, it tells us that our salvation is more nearer now than when we first believed. Every day we hear of senseless acts of violence, random shootings, wars, and wars, rumors of wars, rape and abuse of women and children, and these are just some of the signs of the end times. Have you noticed that the prison population is getting younger and younger, and the level of crimes are getting more violent and horrendous?

Jesus is on His way back and time is no longer on our side. We actually have less time today than we had yesterday. You are going to have to decide if you are going to use this time wandering around the same old mountain or are you going to move to the next level.

When I talk about mountains, I'm not talking about a physical structure. Your mountains are anything that stands in the way of your relationship with Jesus Christ. Your mountains could be your lack of progress, lying, stealing, drugs, alcohol, women or men, lack of commitment, being rebellious against authority, etc. Sin is a mountain and it separates us from God.

One of the problems that Israel had was that her **but** was too big. Yes, I said that her **but** was too big! I hear someone asking, "What's wrong with a big **but**?" Well, I'm glad you asked, because there is a lot wrong with a big **but**! A big **but** will keep you from moving.

For example, Israel would have served the true and living God, **but** instead she wanted to worship the gods of her neighbors. She knew that God sent ten plagues into Egypt and none of them affected the Hebrews, **but** instead she still did not trust God. God fed her manna from heaven when she was hungry, water from the rock when she was thirsty, a cloud to keep her cool by day, a light to see by at night, protection from her enemies, and much more. **But** she still did not believe that God was a provider, because she murmured and complained.

Some of us cannot move because we have a **but** problem! For example, I told my grandmother that I was going to church with her, **but** I don't have a suit to wear. I would go to church with my auntie, **but** I don't have any shoes to wear. I would go to church with my mother, **but** I have to get myself together. I told my wife or girlfriend that I was going to church with her, **but** they stay in church too long. I would go to church, **but** they take up too many offerings. I would give my tithes and offering in the church, **but** I don't know what the preacher is doing with the money. Man, the law didn't have any evidence on me and I wouldn't have had to do any time, **but** my lawyer told me to cop a plea. Here's another one: man I would have paid my child support, **but** I needed some new Jordans and I didn't know what she'd do with the money. Hey, your child has to eat! You eat, don't you? We have been at this mountain long enough and it is time to move.

My brothers, we really have no good excuse for not serving God. The Bible says that the day you hear my voice harden not your heart. It is time for us to make a move.

I would like to share with you some points that I believe will help you move away from your mountains. First, in order for us to move we must admit that we have a problem—and we do have a problem. We all have a sin problem, because all of us have sinned and fall short of the glory of God.

When I lived in Atlanta, I worked at the Georgia Mental Health Institute as a chaplain. While I was there I worked on a drug and alcohol unit. I would go to Alcoholic Anonymous or Cocaine Anonymous meetings so that I could help my clients better. One of the first things they stressed in the meetings is that you have to admit that you are an addict and have a problem before you can recover. Jesus told the Pharisees that if they were whole that they did not a physician (Matt. 9:12). Own up to what you have done and who you are, then seek to change and do better.

The second point is that you must become men of God. You cannot be successful productive men of God until you become saved men. You must have Jesus in your life as your Lord and Savior. You have tried everything else, now it's time to give Jesus a try. He has not left you. Behold, I stand at the door and knock, and if anyone hears my voice

I will come in to him and dine with him (Rev. 3:20). Jesus wants to be a part of your life so much. He is just waiting on you to let Him into your heart.

The third point is that you must study your word. Learn all that you can about Jesus. Join a Bible study group. Learn how to serve God while you are here. Form a relationship with Him. Learn His word and let the Word of God grow in you. Memorize scriptures that will help you go through. You know all of the words to the latest hip-hop songs. You know all the names of the artist like Nicki Manaj, Trey Sonz, Kanye West, Snookie, JWOW, Little Bow Wow, Jay Z, Cee Lo Green, Rhianna, Beyonce, Tupac, Snoop Dog, and others. You know all the names of players in the NBA and NFL but you don't know a single scripture. Learn all that you can while you are in here. Get in school and learn all the trades that the state has to offer. This will help you to become more marketable when you get out.

The fourth point is that you must change the way you think. You need a change of mind. If you want to accomplish anything meaningful, have the faith to believe that you can achieve it. You must believe that you can change without the **buts.** Get rid of the **buts**.

Renew your mind. The Bible says, Let this mind be in you which was also in Christ Jesus (Phil. 2:5). Paul tells us not to conform to this world but be transformed by the renewing of your mind, that you may prove what is that good and acceptable and perfect will of God (Romans 12:2). If we are going to be effective in the kingdom of God, we must be spiritually mature. Spiritual maturity is doing what is right without being told to do so.

Finally, my brothers stay away from negative-speaking people. Associate yourself with people who want to better themselves and change their behavior. Speak a word of change into your lives. Remember that death and life are in the power of the tongue (Proverbs 18:21). Do all that you can to please God. When a man's ways please the Lord, he makes even his enemies to be at peace with him (Proverbs 16:7).

Don't be like Israel, who was always murmuring, complaining, rebellious, and disobedient to God. Choose today to move away from your mountains and make a change in your life. See yourselves as changed men, moving on to a higher level in Christ. Put Him first in your life and He will give you the strength to move away from any mountain.

See yourselves as being the righteousness of God, being new creatures, being the head and not the tail. See yourselves as being drug free, alcohol free, tobacco free, free from high blood pressure, sugar diabetes, cancer, gout, or any other affliction. See yourselves as healthy beings. See yourselves as being beautifully and wonderfully made, men after God's own heart. See yourselves as being who the Bible says you are and doing what this Bible says that you can do.

See yourselves working in the church, serving God, praising God, worshipping God, obeying God's Word, living right, living holy, living saved, being cheerful givers, paying tithes and doing all that you can to please Him. My brothers, see yourselves as being loving husbands and caring, responsible fathers, teaching your sons and daughters to be honest citizens and obeying the law. It is time to move.

11

Good News for the Offender

If you feel that there must be more to the world than what you see passing before your cell every day, then you are correct. There is much, much more to life, even more than you can imagine. You can start a new life today whether you are in prison or out. God loves you, and you can begin your new life with Christ immediately. You do not have to wait until you get out. You can live a life of freedom right where you are.

Yes, the jails and prisons are full of criminals, and so is the rest of the world. The free world is also full of criminals, who were born in sin. But our Savior Jesus Christ came into this world to pay a debt that we owed and could not pay. He actually paid a sin debt that He did not owe that we could not pay.

You may have been discouraged, angry, confused, frustrated with yourself and wanted to give up on life. You tried to figure it all out, to no avail. You know that there has to be an answer, but you just aren't finding it. You lie awake at night with tears rolling down your cheeks, while trying to muffle the echo of your pain, because it would be so unmanly to let your cellmate know that you are crying. You have worn that iron man or woman façade for so long that you even fooled yourself into believing that it is real.

Today, there is good news! Jesus Christ gave you permission to take off the mask and throw away the façade. Yes, you can stop pretending now, because there is a power greater than you and even the warden. It is available to you only if you ask. Jesus understands your pain, and He is willing to give you a chance for a brand new life in Him. Salvation is a free gift that Jesus is waiting for you to receive.

The good news is that Jesus really does want to become a part of your life, if only you allow it to happen. He will not force Himself into your life, but He will come in if you let Him. Open up your hearts and let Him in today.

Jesus took our sin problems to the cross and we can believe and receive that by faith. We can live a Spirit-filled life, totally liberated and free from spiritual bondage. This can be done by embracing and recognizing God's love.

No matter what you have done, no matter what your crime has been in the past, no matter what condition you find yourself in, you can gain strength and confidence in the love than God has for you today. When you really embrace God's love, it will empower you to face all of your life's challenges.

As you except Christ into your heart, you are justified by faith, which gives you peace with God through our Lord Jesus Christ. You are declared righteous before Him. We are then allowed to stand before God and rejoice in the hope of the glory of God (Romans 5:1-2).

In our past life, we were disappointed by so many persons and things. The good news is that we can rejoice because our future hope will not be disappointing or unfulfilled. We can have confidence in this because God's love is poured out in our hearts by the Holy Spirit (Romans 5:5). We will never be disappointed or ashamed.

As believers, we must continue daily to have steadfast confidence in the love of God. When we build our confidence in God's love, we disarm Satan's attempt to tempt us. This also frees us to be about our Father's business.

The good news is that God placed talents, worth, and abilities within you. It is time for you to realize that you no longer have to live a life full of emptiness. Put your trust in God who will give you a desire to rise above your circumstances.

The good news is that although you have had loses of your children, family, or self-respect, you can live again. You can go on by the power of His spirit and the beauty of His strength.

Stop taking a negative inventory of your life. You do not have to be consumed by your losses and you do not have to live in perpetual guilt or shame. It does not matter, because you cannot undo what you have done. But the good news is that God already declared you not guilty. When you were once down to nothing, as good as dead, written off, told that you would never amount to anything, you can live again.

The good news is that God is always there for you and nothing can come against you. What shall we then say to these things? If God be for us, who can be against us? (Romans 8:31).

The good news is that you no longer have to worry about what people will say about your past. Continue to trust in God. No weapon that is formed against thee shall prosper, and every tongue that shall rise against thee in judgment thou shall condemn. This is the heritage of the servant of the Lord, and their righteousness is of me, said the Lord (Isaiah 54:17).

The good news is that you can know without any doubt that God does love you unconditionally. He did not spare His only Son Jesus. God loves us just the way we are, but the good news is that He also loved us so much that He could not just leave us the way we are. But God commended His love toward us, in that, while we were yet sinners, Christ died for us (Romans 5:8).

Remember, yes you did what you did because of the bad choices you made. Yes, you broke the hearts of family, friends, and loved ones. Yes, you may or may not have been rejected because of your choices. But the good news is that God can lift the wings of your sail and allow you to soar. If you want to make it you can. But they that wait upon the Lord shall renew their strength; they shall mount up with wings as eagles; they shall run, and not be weary; they shall walk, and not faint (Isaiah 40:31).

The good news is that you can turn your life around if you are willing. All throughout history, people were locked up, but it did not keep them down. Many were imprisoned who committed no crimes.

In the Bible Joseph committed no crime, but he was thrown into a pit by his own brothers. Later he was taken to Egypt and was imprisoned there after being accused by the pharaoh's wife. He later rose up to become the second most powerful person in Egypt besides the pharaoh. Joseph became a savior to the whole entire nation of Israel. Jeremiah committed no crime, but he was also thrown into a pit. He was one of the major prophets of the Old Testament.

In the New Testament, John the Baptist was the forerunner of Jesus. He also baptized Jesus. He committed no crime, yet he was placed in prison and was finally beheaded. Peter, one of Christ's disciples, committed no crime but he was jailed several times. Paul and Silas went to jail for preaching the word of Christ. The Apostle Paul, who was one of the world's greatest missionaries and evangelists, spent most of his time in prison or under house arrest. He wrote almost half of the New Testament books.

Dr. Marin Luther King Jr. was imprisoned for his non-violent civil rights protests and for speaking out against racism, bigotry, hatred, and segregation. He received the Nobel Peace Prize and numerous other prestigious awards. Today a national holiday has been named in his honor. Nelson Mandela spent thirty years in prison, like Dr. King, for his stand against apartheid in South Africa. He later became the first Black African President of South Africa.

The good news is that there are some real ex-offenders who committed some serious and not so serious crimes who served their sentences and turned their lives around, according to an Internet article in *Business Insider*.

Kevin Mitnick, a former computer hacker, was on the FBI's Most Wanted List. He was a fugitive for three years. Arrested in 1995 and released in 2002, Mitnick has since opened up his own security firm, helping other companies with security issues.

Georgia Durante was once known as the Kodak Summer Girl. She was a famous model who married into a Mafia family and became a getaway driver. After her release, she turned her life around and started her own stunt-driving company.

Frank William Abagnale was a world famous con man by the age of twenty-one, writing over 2.5 million dollars in bad checks. In his past he successfully posed as an airplane pilot, doctor, lawyer, and college professor. He served five years in a French prison. He currently owns his own fraud consulting business.

Kweisi Mfume made several trips to jail. He lost his mother to cancer at the age of sixteen, ran with a gang, and became a leader. He dropped out of high school and fathered five children. At some point in his life, he decided to turn his life around by enrolling in college. He received a degree from Johns Hopkins University, was elected to the Baltimore City Council, Congress, and later became president of the NAACP.

Charles Colson, former Special Counsel for President Richard Nixon pleaded guilty to obstruction of justice in the Watergate scandal. He served seven months in the Federal Prison Camp located at Maxwell Air Force Base in Montgomery, Alabama. Colson accepted Christ while incarcerated and turned his life around. After his release, he helped organize the Prison Fellowship. Today, Prison Fellowship has impacted thousands of prisoners across the nation. Colson died on March 31, 2012.

Judge Greg Mathis often talks about his involvement in gangs during his youth. He went to jail at the age of seventeen and, after his mother was diagnosed with cancer, made a decision to turn his life around. He got his G.E.D., attended Eastern Michigan University, and then on to law school. He has been a popular TV judge since 1999.

Danny Trejo spent twelve years robbing stores, but he's now an actor playing tough guy roles. Steven Richards spent nine years in prison. He received his college degree while still incarcerated. He also earned a PhD degree from Iowa State University. He later became a professor of criminal justice.

NFL Quarterback Michael Vick spent eighteen months in prison. He currently has his own TV show called *The Michael Vick Project* on BET. Some others who have turned their lives around include Robert Downey Jr., Martha Stewart, Tim Allen, Nicole Richie, Marion Jones, and there are many others whose names will never be known nationally or locally; however, their work speaks for itself. It does not matter how or what society has labeled you; a label can always be changed.

12

Testimonies from Ex-Offenders Who Have Turned Their Lives Around

Henry Lee

Henry Lee is an ex-offender who went to prison in 1984. He spent nearly eighteen years behind bars. He once knew God but admits that he backslid on four different occasions. One of the reasons that he fell from the grace of God was that he did not like the suffering that came with being a Christian.

He went back out into the world and started going in and out of jail. In January of 1993, the state of Texas sentenced him to twenty-five years in prison. During that time, he still had not totally surrendered to God. While in prison, he got caught up in all kinds of criminal behaviors associated with prison. He was involved in gambling, stealing, going through the chow lines two or three times, masturbation, etc.

Henry recalled that on December 25, 1999, Christmas Day, that his unit went on lockdown. A murder occurred on the unit, and everybody was on lockdown. During the lockdown, he began listening to a lot of worldly music on the radio and began to realize how angry and depressed he was getting. That led him to start listening to TBN. On one particular occasion, he began listening to Evangelist Juanita Bynum. She gave her testimony, saying she went through some of the same kinds things that he was going through. He identified with what she was saying. It opened his eyes, and that night, he made a decision to stop running from suffering, and accept by faith what God has for him. From that moment on, Brother Lee invited Jesus Christ into his life.

He started reading his Bible and praying. From this he began to gain a deeper understanding of God. Brother Lee started to realize that one of the biggest things holding him back was the fact that he had unforgiveness in his heart. He realized that he had to forgive if God was going to use him. That deepened his understanding and his relationship with God. He acknowledged that unforgiveness was like a roadblock. Brother Lee knew that he had to forgive everybody who was in his life, whether they did anything to him or not. The key to his breakthrough with God was that he started to forgive. He now encourages other offenders that in order for them to build a godly relationship and stay Christ-like, they have to learn how to forgive. He also encourages them to stay in the Word and stay in prayer.

Brother Lee also stated that he was getting older and facing the future. If you want to face the future with success, you will have to do the opposite of what you were doing. He remembers that the first few days or maybe a week or two after you are release that things will be all right for you. Then after that reality will set in, and this is when you will really have to stay focused on what you are going to do. If you don't stay focused, then all the temptations of the world will come down on you.

Brother Lee said that if ex-offenders make a mistake to just get up and start over again. He states that they will need a strong family support system, because it is much too easy to get back out there in the world without family support. If they don't have families, he said, then get with other Christians who will help them stay focused until they are able to stand on their own two feet.

Today Brother Lee is an active member of the Joy and Peace Prison Ministry. He met Overseer Sadie Elliot in 2007, at a trusty camp on the Stringfellow Unit outside of Houston, Texas. He was released in 2010 and just recently announced his calling into the preaching ministry.

Debra Williams

Debra Williams went to prison in 1998 and spent fifteen years incarcerated. When she was released in May of 2012, Debra entered the Community Re-entry Network Program (CRNP). This was a twelve week re-entry program sponsored by the City of Houston Department of Health and Human Services. She was one of the graduate speakers during their graduation ceremony.

Debra encourages offenders and ex-offenders to surrender to God. Give up everything that you thought would make you better, because you can't do it on your own. Have a will to weather the storms of life. Have faith in God that He will bring you through. Stand on your faith and keep doing the next right thing. She states that although temptations will come, remember the pain of the past.

Debra admits that she was the model for *Diary of a Mad Black Woman*. She was a very mad woman. In 2004, she had a spiritual walk with a prison ministry called Kiros. It was at that time that she finally met Jesus and surrendered totally to Him. That spiritual walk was a new experience for her and she has never been the same since. She was at her bottom, and that is where she met Christ after losing everything and everybody, including herself. From that moment on, Debra began to read and study the Bible for herself.

The Christian people that she met had her lost and confused. After going to the church for help, she only went away abused sexually, verbally, and emotionally. But the day that she met the king, her whole life changed and she gladly accepted the change.

Debra was abused even in prison. It is important for women to know that none of us came from an ideal family. You may have experienced verbal, physical, emotional, and sexual abuse. You may have come from a family of poverty, rage, drug and alcohol addiction, divorce, etc. You may have struggled with low self-esteem, failed marriages, loneliness, depression, anxiety, anger issues, and dysfunctional parenting. But in spite of having a bad start, it does not mean that you cannot have a great finish.

According to Debra, your lives today can be happier than yesterday. It is better to burn out for Christ than rust out for Satan. You cannot walk and remain in the same place. You are either going to go forward or you are going to go backward. I can do all things through Christ that strengthens me (Phil. 4:13).

Debra is currently working for the Houston Rapid Transit (HRT). When the whole world said no, HRT gave her a chance.

Nevada Strange

Nevada Strange spent thirty years of her life on paper and five years behind bars. She was on probation for twenty years and on parole for ten years. Probation for her was not an easy task, and it was much stricter than parole. During her probation period, she was not to go to any clubs. She had to stay away from criminal activities, give clean urine tests, couldn't lie, had to pay restitution fees, and avoid other people who were on parole. It limited her social life, affected her family, and loved ones, because if they were on parole she could not be around them. She was also prohibited from carrying a gun. Finding a job was also difficult for her. Once she found a job, her P.O. (Probation Officer) could visit at any time, and that could be embarrassing. She always had to be careful of the places she visited because a fight could break out and that would mean trouble for her. She had to avoid any place or situation that would jeopardize her freedom.

Although parole was not as hard for Nevada to follow, she still had to do whatever was asked of her. Her parole had to be completed. It affected her financially because if she was working she still had to pay fees including her other bills. Sadly to say if the employer knew that you were on parole, they could actually pay you less than minimum wages and get away with it, especially if they know you needed a job.

Before she accepted Christ into her life she was always upset with an I-didn't-want-to-be-there attitude, and it showed. She didn't want to leave her drug and alcoholic life alone. One day, Nevada came to realize that she was playing Russian roulette with her life. She thought that she could get away with everything, that she could manipulate the system, and that the rules of life did not apply to her because she believed that she was running the show. She was miserable and wanted others to be miserable, too.

Nevada finally had a spiritual awakening. She discovered that she was not going anywhere. She began to pray for forgiveness and asked Christ into her life. She started attending church on the unit, worked in the chaplain's office, conducted Bible study, became a trustee, and was a member of the battered and abused women group.

When Jesus came into Nevada's life, she started a 7:00 p.m. nightly prayer from her cell. She was a prayer warrior, and people from all walks of life and every race would come to her for prayer. The nightly prayer soon evolved into morning and prayer after lunch as well. She would lead her dorm in prayer and sometimes, even the guards would join in.

Now, Nevada encourages others not to look at their situation but to look to God. She knows He and only He can deliver them from any situation. For those that didn't get visits, she encouraged them to get out of their cells, go to church, and keep trusting God.

On January 10, 2013, Nevada was given a letter of character issued by her attorney to the courts. The purpose of the letter was to help get her criminal record expunged. He states that from the moment that he first met her there was something different about her. His first visit was one that he would never forget. After his first visit he was convinced that she was framed, and he was willing to work with her.

He admitted that Nevada did something that took him totally by surprise. She began to pray for him. He acknowledged that the words that came from her mouth were not of this world. Her prayer overwhelmed him. He was both stunned and blessed by the peace that came over him. Her lawyer stated that Nevada encountered Jesus. She was given incredible grace and has been an inspiration to everyone she meets. She doesn't have to even open her mouth in that her very presence is a blessing to all that she encounters. Her faith is not her own; it is the spirit and faith of Christ in her that speaks louder than any words that she could ever utter. She is an inspiration and blessing.

Nevada is a volunteer in the Joy and Peace Prison Ministry. She currently visits and speaks to other inmates who come through the court system. She also has various speaking engagements around the city. Her advice to them is to avoid getting caught up in worldly things because God wants to use them.

Lonnie Provo

I first met Lonnie when he became involved in the Evangelist Outreach Prison Ministry, a volunteer prison ministry started by my deceased husband. Lonnie was one of our first volunteers. We traveled to Gatesville, Texas, to the Gatesville Prison's women's unit every second Sunday. Later, we sometimes traveled to Dickerson, Texas, to Carole Young Medical facility on first the Sunday of the month. Lonnie was very faithful and committed.

Then one day, without a warning, Lonnie walked away from the ministry and his marriage. I became very angry with Satan because of this. We lost contact for years. We recently reconnected while doing prison ministry at Pam Lyncher State Jail. We were so excited to see each other. Today he has been reconciled back to God and pastoring a church. This is his story.

"My name is Lonnie R. Provo. I am fifty-eight years old now. I grew up as any normal little child. My mother and father both worked and did the best they could to raise four children. I was the oldest of the four. My mother and father married when he was twenty-three; he was two years older than my mother. We were a happy family, even though no one in the family knew Jesus Christ as Lord or even Savior.

"My biggest troubles began at the age of twelve. My mother and father separated at that time, and that turned into a divorce. At the age of twelve, I began to hate my mother because of the divorce.

"I ran away from her to live with my grandmother and my dad. I wanted to live with my grandmother because I could get away with things with her that I could not get away with my mother.

"By the time I reached eighteen years old, I was in prison. I felt my whole world had come to an end. In June of 1973, I was sentenced to fifteen years in the Texas Department of Corrections. My dreams of going to college and possibly playing football in the NFL were all gone.

"I can't remember how, but in prison at that time church was out of the question. I attended only one church service while in prison the first time. I developed a hatred for God and that hatred grew stronger daily. I served five and a half years in prison at that time and there was only one man who could come near me with a Bible, Mr. Harry Higgins. As I threw Bibles in the trash cans, he would tell me that I was living on the prayers of my mother.

"I hated her just as much as I hated God! I cursed God and I cursed my mother. I blamed God and I blamed my mother. I blamed the white man for all the bad that happened to me in my life! Be not deceived; God is not mocked. Whatsoever a man sows in life that shall he also reap.

"I was filled with hatred! After being released from prison at the age of twenty-four, from a fifteen-year sentence, I just knew I arrived. I thought I was on top of the world. I was released from prison on March 17, 1979.

"I still hated God and my mother! In November of that same year, God began to challenge my thought process about Him being real or not. I said, man I made it without you in prison, and I can do the same in the free world. I said, I don't need you.

"Well, on December 24, 1979, I was arrested again for robbery. I was on my way back to TDCJ, this time with a fresh twenty-five-year sentence. I thought, how can I do twenty-five years when I had just finished five and a half on a fifteen years! I stayed on the streets for seven months, and now I was back in prison. I said to myself that day, you didn't stay out of prison long enough to use a can of shaving cream.

"As I thought, I cried out, I need! One has to understand that I always prided myself in the fact that I didn't need Him. Well, one night I read the poem "Footprints in the Sand." I cried a river of tears that night. I served eight and a half years on the Darrington Prison Unit, all eight and a half years, I spent them as a Christian. I was released from prison in December of 1988.

"Today, I have been out of prison for twenty-five years. I am off of parole. I go back into the prisons now as a preacher. I am the founder and pastor of the Shekinah Glory Christian Center. I am also the founder and director of Shekinah Glory Ministries International Incorporated. Under that ministry umbrella is Keep Your Head to the Sky Prison Ministry. God has also blessed me with a Prison Radio Program "Oasis," of which I am also founder and director. I am also blessed to be able to help offenders with housing and a fresh start upon being release from prison."

Jerry Graham said in his book, *Where Flies Don't Land*, "Every day is not easy," but with the Lord Jesus Christ as being the head of my life, I have life and I have it more abundantly (John 10:10). I have been blessed to do volunteer prison ministry with Lonnie and he is truly a devoted man of God.

Bishop Eugene Tannehill

Bishop Eugene Tannehill is one of the most incredible, remarkable, Spirit-filled persons that I have ever had the pleasure of meeting. I first met him when he came to visit a local church in Humble, Texas. During that time he was a guest speaker at the church. He was invited to come on our unit as a special guest and speak to the men at the Pam Lynchner State Jail. Chaplain Donald Lacy introduced him as a unique person that would really be a blessing to all, including the volunteers. That brief introduction did not do him real justice. The man was absolutely amazing with an amazing story to tell.

Bishop Tannehill spent fifty years incarcerated in the Angola Louisiana State Penitentiary. It houses five thousand inmates and is one of the largest maximum security prisons in Louisiana. A documentary film entitled *The Farm* highlighted his life along with five other inmates. I pray that one day some filmmaker will make a full-length film about his true life story. It will truly be a blessing for offenders, ex-offenders, and those involved in criminal activities or young people in general, especially Black males. Bishop Tannehill was incarcerated longer than anyone in the Louisiana state's prison history.

He dropped out of school in the seventh grade, and was convicted of murder in 1960 at the age of twenty. When I first met him, he was seventy-five year old and he looked to be around sixty. God really preserved him. During the course of a robbery gone badly, he committed a murder. He stated that he thought the Pentecostal preacher had some money. He stabbed him and robbed him of about three dollars.

While Bishop Tannehill was in prison, he stated that he witnessed every kind of prison violence imaginable. By the grace of God, he survived the prison environment. During his incarceration, he became a trusted-gun carrying prison guard. In his early years, he became a born-again Christian and "bishop" of the church in prison.

He was released from Angola Prison in August 2007. The then Governor Kathleen Blanco commuted his life sentence following the recommendations from the Louisiana State Board of Pardon and Parole. Bishop Tannehill stated that at his hearing, Governor Blanco actually turned her head as she signed his release. Bishop Tannehill believed that she was being influenced by Satan. He asked God to forgive her and was able to move on. He knew he had to overlook her actions because everyone was so proud and happy for him.

Bishop also testified that while he was in prison that the Lord told him that he would live in Brooklyn, New York. He didn't know anyone in Brooklyn and had never been there before in his life. The Lord also told him that he would one day be a millionaire. Following his commuted sentence, he was released to the custody of the Brooklyn Tabernacle Church in Brooklyn, New York.

One of Bishop's main goals is to help other young men stay out of prison and avoid criminal activities. Since his release, God blessed him with a beautiful wife. He currently travels, going in and out of prisons, speaking at prison conferences and workshops, churches, or any organizations that will give him an open forum. He has also appeared on TBN.

Bishop Tannehill stated that Angola was once known as the "bloodiest prison in America" and the most dangerous and violent prison in the country. Today, it is a much reformed institution because of the reform movement that was instituted by Warden Burl Cain, his staff, and the inmates. In his book entitled *Cain Redemption*, Warden Cain talks about how Bishop Tannehill had such a profound spiritual influence on his life. He professes that Eugene Tannehill is his Bishop. I found that Bishop Eugene Tannehill was an amazing man. The first time I met him, my first thoughts were that he was just another self-appointed man trying to gain recognition as a bishop. I was so wrong because he truly is a man of God, and the inmates as well as the volunteers were blessed by his testimony. When he finished, the men were moved to tears and could hardly let him go. None of them would be the same after listening to his testimony.

13

Parent's Testimony

Dr. Earline Allen

Dr. Earline Allen, Founder of Immanuel Bible College and District Missionary, is an evangelist, author, lecturer, pastor's wife, mother, church mother, and Church of God in Christ historian. She is also the mother of Samuel Ray Allen. Sammy, as he is called, was reared in the Church of God in Christ as a preacher's kid and is currently incarcerated. He spent the last twenty plus years of his life going in and out of prison. As a child, Sammy probably attended church four or five times a week, including Sundays.

He was a college graduate with a degree in business, honest, hardworking on his job, and a good and faithful church worker. He worked on one job thirty years, driving a bus for METRO. He owned a home, fine furniture, nice clothes, jewelry, two cars and a truck, and never missed a family holiday. He was a family man.

Sammy's life started to change after he was involved in a serious bus accident. He ruined his spine and started taking pain killers. He had surgery but it didn't relieve his back pain. As far as Dr. Allen remembers, this was actually the start of his drug addiction. He did receive a settlement from the accident, but he was so addicted that he was withdrawing hundreds of dollars at a time to support his habit.

Eventually, Sammy started to spiral downward. He lost his wife and family. He was hurt by the divorce, angry, bitter, and got worse and worse. Then he started to get arrested. The first time, he got arrested, Dr. Allen stated that she was very disappointed with him because he was not a youngster; he was a man in his forties.

Dr. Allen could not believe that this was happening to her son since he was doing so well in his livelihood. The first time that she actually saw him in handcuffs, she said that it nearly killed her because she was so hurt. She used to visit him regularly until he started going in and out prison so many times.

While Sammy was incarcerated he would kick his habit, but as soon as he got out he would return to his same old neighborhood and get caught up in the same cycle all over again.

Dr. Allen prayed hard that God would turn her son around. She did not want him to get killed in the old neighborhood. When he would come to church, the church people would always try to probe into his business and he would stop coming.

His mother's constant prayer was that God would put someone in his life that would encourage him to turn his life around. She stated that when he got out he seemed like he wanted to do better, but the drugs had a strong hold on him. He is now being tested for prostate cancer and that weighs heavy on her heart. She wonders if she can ever trust him again. When he gets out, there's always the feeling of uncertainty and the question of "How long will he stay out?"

It troubled Dr. Allen how Sammy got started on the drugs. She always heard that a mother never gives up. Today, she knows that it's true. There were many days that she would try to rationalize her son's behavior. Naturally, she would ask why me, why now, or how did he come to this? Growing up, Sammy and his father had a rocky relationship, and she often wondered if this could have had something to do with his rebellion and drug abuse.

Dr. Allen's advice to parents is to never, give up on your child. If you know God, you don't give up because there is hope. You can be like the woman who went to the unjust judge. Hold on to your faith. No problems are too big for God. Sometimes, things may get worse before they get better. If you are faithful, God will bring you out of your situation. When it looks like your child is gone for good, just keep on praying. You may find yourself struggling but believe God like Abraham. The Bible says that he staggered not at the promise of God but held on. Sometimes, it may take a long time, and you may wonder if it is ever going to happen.

Mother Allen tells parents not to focus on their sunset, but focus on the dawning of a new day. You will have challenges that will come to slow you down, retard your progress, and steal your joy. Stay focused on your destiny and never give up.

Ralph Wells

Ralph Wells is a retired public school teacher, former teacher at C. H. Mason Bible College and Institute, District Superintendent, former Chairman of the Jurisdictional Assembly, currently co-chairman of the Jurisdictional Assembly, and pastor.

When Pastor Wells found out that his son was using drugs, he confronted him. His first confrontation was hard on him, because he was not just a pastor but a Pentecostal pastor. He admits that at first he was in denial. He did not believe that one of his own children could be involved in drugs, knowing how hard he preached against drugs and alcohol abuse. When he confronted his son he was in for an unexpected shock. His son admitted to him that he was homosexual.

There was a heated exchange of words and his son stated that his dad did not know anything about him. His son accused him of being the reason that he was a homosexual. Pastor Wells was actually stunned and asked what he meant. He responded by saying that he liked men. First, he was talking about drugs, and then he learned that his only son was a homosexual. He was so shocked that he walked away. Pastor Wells now realizes that the signs were there all the time, but he ignored them.

For months, he began to fast and pray. He confronted his son again, and this time he had an open conversation about what was really going on. The son admitted that all of his life, everybody always expected him to measure up to his father. He felt that he could not measure up to the high expectations that his father set for him. He felt more comfortable talking to males.

Pastor Wells felt extremely guilty about this revelation. During that time, some of his neighbors were homosexual men selling crack. He believes that this is where his son's addiction started. One thing lead to another and for a long time he felt responsible for what happened. However, after much fasting, praying, and studying, he came to the conclusion that this was an individual choice. It was at this time that he really started to reach out to his son. Pastor Wells admits that he once went into a crack house and took his son out.

Over a period of years, his son's drug problem would come and go. The last time that he was arrested, he was not high but he was caught with a pipe. He served eighteen months on a three-year sentence. That last trip to prison got his attention, and he started attending church and allowing God to work in his life while he experienced his healing grace. Today, he has his own business as an independent mortician and hairstylist. He is the father of three girls and one son. He is a responsible father and doing well, totally committed to serving God faithfully. He is also a member of the adult choir, brotherhood, and an inspirational speaker to young people.

These are all testimonies from real people who have agreed to share their stories.

14

My Story

I saved my story for last. I really struggled with whether I would include it or not. I concluded that it needed to be told. There are several reasons that I struggle with telling my own story. First of all, it was one area of my life that I wish never happened. It was so painful for me that I actually blocked it out of my memory.

I was hurt and I did not want to bring that hurt up again. However, I did not block out all of the details, but I blocked out a lot. I first started to remember when my son went to prison for the second time. I was so angry with him that I said that I was not going to waste my time going to visit him or send him any more money. He supposedly went to jail for something that he did not do. But when I thought about it some more, God reminded me of the painful memories of my past that I tried all of my adult life to forget.

When I was in my early twenties and a student at Texas Southern University (TSU) and member of the Black Student Union (BSU), I was arrested with a group of fellow members and charged with possession of explosives. I was walking across the campus one day, after being released from class early. The BSU members saw me and asked for a ride to go pick up something. I knew that it was not drugs, but I didn't question it any further. The police surrounded us and we were arrested and taken into custody.

From that moment on, my life became a living hell right here on earth. My life literally took a three hundred and sixty-degree turn within minutes. I thought it was a nightmare and that I would wake up and the nightmare would all be over and that I would return to my happy life as a student trying to prepare for my future. I was so wrong because it was not over, it was just beginning.

I actually knew what it meant to become a victim of circumstance, because now I was one. Most persons locked up will state that they are innocent, but I felt that I was not guilty of the crime that they were charging me with. The police arrest was actually a setup. I was not a part of the purchase; however, I was treated the same.

We were released on bail. Before the trial date, however, I left town. I jumped bail and did not show up for my trial. I felt in my heart that since the police set me up and that they would send me to prison for twenty-five years of my life. The idea of that happening was not a part of my future.

I was young and mostly frightened. I left Texas and became a fugitive from justice. My travel decision landed me on the FBI's most wanted list, something that I am not proud of, but it happened. I traveled around a bit and even changed my identity. While living in San Francisco. I was arrested on an assault charge but it was dropped. My fingerprints were in the FBI's database and I was arrested and charged with interstate flight to avoid prosecution. This actually turned out to be a blessing in disguise. First of all, the moment it happened, I literally felt that a heavy weight had been lifted off of my shoulders. Secondly, while waiting to go to trial, I waived my right to extradition. The state of Texas had forty-five days to come to San Francisco and take me back to Texas. Somehow, or for other reasons, they decided that I was not worth the expense, so they refused to come and get me. This was my blessing, because the state of California dropped the charges and my record was cleared with no conviction. I truly experienced him that day as a lawyer in the courtroom. For me it was more than just a song, but it was real, thank God. After serving forty-five days waiting for extradition, I was now free to go home. When I was processed out, the clothes that I had worn when I was arrested were falling off of me. I had lost a lot of weight worrying. I don't recommend this weight lost program. I went through a period of anger and depression. I still could not figure out what was happening to my life and why it was happening.

This whole experience left me bitter, angry, frustrated, depressed, disgusted, and very unhappy. It was the worst period of my life. I should have been relieved and excited about having that burden lifted, but I was utterly miserable. During that time, I was married to an alcoholic and drug abuser. He was little help to me, and I was miserable and completely disgusted with my life.

My anger had been building for a long time, even long before I was arrested. I had to change my name and I was living under an alias. I could not contact my family; and I did not know who to blame for all the things that I went through. I was always angry. I was like a time bomb just waiting to explode at any moment. At that time, turning to God was nowhere on my agenda. During that time in my life, I did not realize that turning to God was even a remote possibility.

I started to try to get my life back in some sort of order by going to school to become dental assistant, but my penned up anger was still there. One day when I was supposed to take a test, I came in under the influence. I was cheating and I got caught. I stormed out of there and destroyed a lot of dental equipment along the way. Of course, that was the end of my dental career. When I reflect back on what I did, I realize now that I made some very stupid moves in my life, but God was still right there watching over me because it could have been a whole lot worse.

My life was falling completely apart. I was not serving God at the time; besides that, I felt that he was the last person to have had anything to do with what I was going through. Of course, I was oh so wrong. I failed to realize that He and He alone is always in complete and absolute control of my life.

I grew up loving Jesus. I was an honest person. I did not steal or try to cheat people. I treated people fairly and I was a morally good person except for the fact that I sold marijuana. I was in total darkness and on my way to hell. But I thank God so much that He turned me around and brought me out of my ignorance.

Eventually, I got saved and received Jesus Christ into my life as my Lord and Savior. A child evangelist named Ardella Portis, who has since gone on to glory, led me to the Lord. I learned so much from Mother Portis. Before I actually met her, I seriously misjudged her. My ex-husband wanted me to meet her. My first thoughts about her were not very nice. However, from the moment that I met her, my life has not been the same since. I immediately fell in love with her spirit. The more that I began to interact with her, the more she taught me about Jesus. I was so impressed with her knowledge of the Word of God. I started following her to the sanctified church and I later joined.

I graduated from San Diego State University with a bachelor of arts degree. I earned a masters of divinity degree from Interdenominational Theological Center (ITC) in Atlanta, Georgia, and a Doctor of Ministry Degree from Houston Graduate School of Theology

By now my life totally changed. I was saved, delivered, happy, and my sins were forgiven. After graduating from ITC, I continued to reside in Atlanta. I worked at the Georgia Mental Health Institute as a chaplain intern.

Near the end of my internship, I felt God was leading me away from Atlanta. It was also around this time that my son was starting to act out. He was being truant from school. I decided that we would move to Houston. I was offered a chaplain internship at M. D. Anderson Cancer Center. My family was happy that I moved back. While I was a chaplain helping others get through their pain and the issues associated with cancer, I needed help with my troubles. My son started getting in more trouble and was eventually sent to an alternative school.

During my internship, I got to experience the power of God in a brand new way. I got to know Him on a different level. For about fifteen years, I lived my life thinking that I was no longer a wanted person. Someone forgot to inform the state of Texas, however, that my charges had been dropped and I was no longer wanted.

One night, I was traveling home and I was pulled over by an unmarked police vehicle for a broken tail light. When they pulled me over and checked my license, it showed that I had a warrant and was still a wanted person. I was arrested and taken to jail. But this time, I knew Jesus and the entire experience was different.

I definitely knew that this was a mistake, that God was in control, that He would clear this up for good, and that this would no longer be a thorn in my flesh. God knew that my name needed to be cleared. It is amazing how when you find yourself in a situation and know beyond a doubt that God is in control of things regardless of the outcome, your outlook is completely different.

I knew without a doubt that He would bring me out and that He would get the glory. It was more than just a cliché or a song for me. It was a life-changing experience. I was still a babe in Christ, but I still knew that God was in control.

My whole experience was different. Obviously, I was upset and disappointed about being arrested. It started to feel like a nightmare was starting to evolve all over again. I just knew that that part of my life was dead and buried, not to surface again.

I wasn't incarcerated long before I went to court. The charges were dropped and I was ordered to pay a fine. This time, I didn't leave the courts angry or bitter. I left praising

God. I was confident beyond a shadow of a doubt that God was in this with me. He certainly proved to me that He would never leave me nor forsake me.

I returned to work feeling very ashamed and embarrassed. My supervisor and peers, however, were very supportive of me. They were truly a community of grace and that was just what I needed. They were all white and they accepted me back just as I was, although I still felt that I was tarnished. I felt that I would be stigmatized, but I wasn't.

We were supposed to share in a group setting. For the first several days, I didn't say anything because I still felt embarrassed by the whole incident. I was actually harder on myself than my peers were. When I finally did begin to share, it felt like a load had been lifted.

This entire experience really taught me about the power of forgiveness. I had to learn how to forgive from my heart and not just from my mouth. I learned that forgiveness was not for the law enforcement officers, but it was for my healing and restoration. My healing did not occur overnight. It was a process for me. Today, I can say the healing is complete.

I highly respect and appreciate the work that law officers do. Their lives can be in constant danger. My prayers are constantly with them and their families. Our children should be taught to respect law officers. God gave them authority to enforce the laws of the land and we must obey them.

I have currently dedicated about eighteen years of my life to prison ministry. It is something that I truly enjoy doing. I have rarely missed an opportunity to minister in the jails or prisons. I know that this is my calling in ministry. God had been preparing me for this all along.

My first volunteer jail ministry experience was in Atlanta. I went into the Fulton County Jail where we ministered to female inmates. I spent six years going to the women's unit in Gatesville, Texas. During that time, I also went to the South Texas Regional Medical Facility in Dickerson, Texas. This facility houses inmates who are too sick to remain on regular units throughout the state.

I have been actively involved with several prison ministry teams. They included New Hope Church of God in Christ Jail Ministry; Evangelist Outreach Prison Ministry, which is the prison ministry that was founded by my deceased husband, the late Dr. R.

C. Robinson; and Mount Rose Church of God in Christ Prison Ministry. I am currently an active member of the Joy and Peace Prison Ministry founded by Overseer Sadie Elliott. I have also gone in as a special guest of other prison ministries.

I know that I cannot erase my past; however, I have come to a place in my ministry where I am no longer ashamed of my past. I don't fully understand all or why what happened did happen, but I know that God was in the plan. We cannot change our past, but the good news is that we don't have to, because our past was nailed to the cross by the blood of Jesus.

When the Holy Spirit leads me, I will share my testimony in the prisons. I let the inmates know that when we repent that God will not hold our past against us. We all have a past, but we do not have to be a prisoner of our past. There is total and absolute freedom in serving Jesus Christ. I am sold out and determined to gain more of Jesus each and every day. My past may have been dismal, but today, I have the promise of a glorious future, living in eternity with my Lord and Savior Jesus Christ. Hallelujah! To God be the glory!

15

Confession of Faith

If you have a child or loved one who is incarcerated or not living a Christ-centered life, I encourage you to make this confession over their lives every day and see God move by faith.

I confess that_____ (loved one) is a new creature in Christ, a changed person. In Christ _____is anointed and a powerful person of God. _____ is a hearer and doer of the Word of God and a channel for His blessings. _____is a peculiar person called out of darkness and into His marvelous light. _____ have put off the old man and put on the new man renewed in the knowledge after the image of Him that created_____. He or she has received the spirit of wisdom and revelation in the knowledge of Him; the eyes of _____ are being enlightened, and _____is not conformed to this world, but transformed by the renewing of _____mind. _____mind is renewed daily by the Word of God.

_____is free and delivered from the bondage of drugs, alcohol tobacco, violence, or any inappropriate activities. He or she is an honest person whose life is lining up with the Word of God. He or she is not without spot or blemish, an intercessor, walking and living in the Word of God, and witnessing to others about the saving grace of Jesus Christ. He or she is a responsible adult, leading their families in worship and taking them to church. _____ is a faithful and committed child of God, washed by the blood of the lamb.

16

Conclusion

Naked and ye clothed me: I was sick and ye visited me; I was in prison and ye came unto me (Matthew 25:36).

One of the most important lessons that I have learned from my son's incarceration is that he can go to God for himself. Nevertheless, the Bible tells us that we are our brother's keeper and we that are strong are to bear the infirmities of the weak (Romans 15:1).

None of our children, whether they were reared in the church or not, are immune from crimes, violence, drug or alcohol addictions, sexual abuse, immortality, etc. We are all sinners and come short of the glory of God.

As parents, we cannot continue to blame ourselves for the bad decisions that our children have made and or will make. I have never taught my son to do wrong. However, I can recall when I first started in prison ministry, I met a man who was in a wheelchair and his own son who was also incarcerated was pushing him. Both men are Christians now. The father admitted that he taught his sons to be criminals. After Jesus came into his life, he regretted it.

When you have reared your children in the best way that you thought was right and in their best interest, then you have nothing to be regretful or ashamed of.

Sometimes, the best lessons they learn are the ones they have to pay for in one way or another. As parents, we must learn to let our child or children go. We can cut the umbilical cord but still love them dearly.

I learned that forgiveness can release us from the stigmatization of having been incarcerated or having a child that has been incarcerated, especially if you are a leader in the church. I had to learn to forgive myself, so that I would not block my blessings or hinder my relationship with God.

We cannot blame the church, the absent parent, financial situation, living conditions, racism, or anything. But we must never give up on our children and we must encourage them to seek God for themselves. They must also learn to be patient, sincerely reconnect with God, repent of their sins, invite Jesus into their lives, stay in the Word, pray, and connect with a Christian fellowship.

Encourage them to put Jesus first in their lives. But seek ye first the kingdom of God, and His righteousness, and all these things shall be added unto you (Matthew 6:33). Remind them that when God is ready for them to be released, He will open the doors and not the parole board. They can still live free for Christ in prison or out of prison. It may take some time for them to realize this, but trust God to do what He does best and He will never fail.

Being incarcerated is hard on a family, especially a mother. Love does cover a multitude of faults. Jesus' sacrificial death on the cross proved that He loved us, dying on the cross to cover our many faults. Saved parents want their children to be saved as well. If we are on our way to heaven, it is obvious for us to want our sons and daughters to go to there, too. We must continue to pray and pray more for our children that they become born again, regenerated, justified, sanctified, reconciled, and redeemed by the power and Spirit of God.

Remember, yes, they have carried us to jails and prisons with them physically, emotionally, and spiritually. Once they are released, the bonds are still not broken because they will still need our help more than ever.

Most women will need extra help. If their children have been taken from them and become a ward of the courts, they will need to prove to the courts that they have been rehabilitated and are responsible mothers. Some may have to show proof of completing a drug or alcohol treatment program. Their urine samples must be drug free. They will have to have suitable employment and a suitable place for them to reside.

Many of these things will not happen overnight, and it will take patience for both the parent and their child. Some may get discouraged, but we must encourage them to remain faithful and continue to trust God. When God is ready, their family will be restored.

Be prepared to help the ex-offender get to the parole office ASAP, as that is their top priority. They will also need clothes, underwear, shoes, etc. Some of them will only own the clothes they have on their backs. They may not fit, may be wrinkled, or outdated. They will also need bus cards so that they can learn to use public transportation. Remember, that it is not your job or your responsibility to take them everywhere they need to go.

The Joy and Peace Prison Ministry does an excellent job helping newly-released offenders with clothes and shoes. The founder, Sister Sadie, does all this from her own pocket. She gets no outside help except for donations. She volunteers in and out of several prison units throughout the Southeast Texas area. She also finds time to do volunteer work in the chaplain's office. She is a Certified Volunteer Chaplain (CVC) in the Texas Department of Criminal Justice (TDJC).

I am also a CVC. Volunteer Prison Ministry has been such a blessing for me. Serving in the prisons or jails is something that I am very passionate about. I just love it. It is very fulfilling and I highly recommend it. It is also a much-needed ministry, since one out of five Black males are in prison. The representation should also be more visible. If you don't feel the need to go, then help support someone who does feel the need. Prison ministry is not for everyone. However, you can be a financial blessing to those who go. Most prison ministries are supported by volunteer participations.

I encourage you to explore the prison ministry as a possible outreach ministry for yourself. Contact your local state's department of criminal justice and they will send you an application. In the state of Texas, an ex-offender who has been out for two years can apply for volunteer prison ministry. Each state will vary and have different requirements. If you don't know of a particular prison ministry, check with the unit chaplains and they will be more than happy to direct you.

Our children are a vital part of who we are. We have carried them in our bodies and our hearts. No matter how much we love them, we simply cannot carry them by ourselves. We need the home, the church, family, and the community. It truly takes a whole village to raise a child.

Through the promises of a righteous Lord, as believers we have hope (Jer. 29:11). God is able to do exceedingly and abundantly above all that we ask or think, according to the power that works in us (Eph. 3:20).

Remember that God in His own time and in His own way, by His own power will bring the light of salvation to our loved one. God's ways are not our ways.

He works and moves on his own timetable. In the meantime, we are to remember that we are His beloved children, and we are to continually trust God and believe with confidence and assurance that He will perform His Word.

Bibliography

Tannehill, Bishop Eugene. Highest Common Denominator. Media Group Website.

Dollar, Creflo A. *Unrooting the Spirit of Fear.* Tulsa, OK: Harrison House, 1994.

Dollar, The Max A Newsletter from C. D. Ministerial Association. Maximize Your Vision. December 2012.

Hogan-Williams, Carole. *S.K.I.P. "Saints Kids in Prison,"* 2009.

Shere, Dennis. *Cain's Redemption.* Chicago: Northfield Publishing, 2005.

Teaching Children Responsibility for Their Learning and Behavior. Fairfax, VA: The Parent Institute. 2007.

10 Ex-Criminals Who Completely Turned Their Careers Around. Business Insider. Pamphlets

God Can Forgive. The Word Among Us Press, 2003.

I Have Decided. Fort Worth, TX: Inmate Discipher Fellowship.

Staying Involved With Your Children While Incarcerated.

National Fatherhood Initiative.

The Worry Disease. Tarpon Springs, FL: Love Press, 2003.

Glossary Of Terms

Cell mate (cellie)—the person or persons with whom you share a cell with.

Johnnie—a sack lunch consisting of a cold sandwich and no extras.

Lockdown—when inmates are confined to a cell. They have no exercise yard, no visitors, and no hot meals. Some cells maybe searched for illegal drugs, weapons, phones, etc. Security is tightened and guards may be armed.

Parole—the release of a convicted offender who has completed part of their sentence. It is based on the principle that the released or parolee can prove he or she has been rehabilitated and can "make good" in society. The paroled has a time period to complete certain terms of their parole, such as reporting to their parole office within the first twenty hours of their release. They may also be required to pay a fee, stay out of trouble, etc. The parole office may visit the parolee's place of residence or work place.

Parolee—the ex-offender or person being released or paroled.

Parole officer (P.O.)—the person to whom the newly released person **must** visit. They will check on the parolee, make home visits, collect fees, urine samples, give job leads, and help the parolee stay focused and out of jail or prison.

Police heat—when the police are checking to see what you are doing, where you are going, or what you have been doing.

Probation—a chance to remain free, or serve a short time given by a judge to the convicted person instead of them going to jail or prison, provided the person stays out of trouble.

Warden—head person in charge of a prison unit.

www.ingramcontent.com/pod-product-compliance
Lightning Source LLC
LaVergne TN
LVHW060207080526
838202LV00052B/4201